That was the absolute best and the absolute worst summer of my life, the summer I turned sixteen.

Sixteen is a weird year. Make it sixteen with your dad off finding himself again—not that he'd been around much even before the divorce—and your mom in remission from ovarian cancer, and you can pretty much figure you're being dumped on from somewhere.

What I didn't figure, and couldn't ever have figured, was how bad it was going to get—and how completely impossible both the bad and the good part would be.

Magic. It's dead, they say. Or never existed.

They aren't looking in the places I fell into, or finding it where I found it, that wonderful and terrible summer.

**Living in Threes**
Copyright © 2014 Judith Tarr
Published by Book View Café Publishing Cooperative

ISBN: 978-1-61138-450-5

Interior illustration by Emily Lyman
Cover design by Leah Cutter

BVC Production team:
Sherwood Smith, Julianne Lee, Vonda N. McIntyre

# Living in Threes

## Judith Tarr

Book View Café
www.BookViewCafe.com

# Other Books by Judith Tarr

**Novels**

Ars Magica
A Wind in Cairo
His Majesty's Elephant

**The Hound and the Falcon**

The Isle of Glass
The Golden Horn
The Hounds of God

Alamut
The Dagger and the Cross

**Forthcoming**

Forgotten Suns

**Collections**

Nine White Horses: Nine Stories of Horses and Magic

**Nonfiction**

Writing Horses: The Fine Art of Getting it Right

**BVC Anthologies**

Beyond Grimm
Breaking Waves
Brewing Fine Fiction
Ways to Trash Your Writing Career
Dragon Lords and Warrior Women
Rocket Boy and the Geek Girls
The Shadow Conspiracy
The Shadow Conspiracy
The Shadow Conspiracy II

# Living in Threes

## Judith Tarr

# Acknowledgments

This book could not have existed without the help of many friends and colleagues.

My agents, Russell Galen and Ann Behar, believed in it enough to let it go—and to encourage me to publish it through Book View Café.

But before that could happen, this happened: a successful Kickstarter, a round 256 backers, and the wherewithal to transform a manuscript into a book.

Thanks to the backers who have made it possible for *Living in Threes* to make its way out into the world:

Cora Anderson, Richard Kirka, Marty Grabien, Gwyndyn Alexander, Kari Sperring, Kathleen G. Seal, Alan Hamilton, Robin Taylor, Marci Ellingwood, Carole Nowicke, Ingrid Emilsson, Lisa Clark, Kit Kerr, Meredith Tarr, Woj, Katja Kasri, Hugh Agnew, Marianne Reddin Aldrich, Val Kondrich, Nancy Kaminski, Kathleen Hanrahan, Robin Marwick, RJ Nicolo, Molly Kalafut, Elizabeth Bennefeld, Michael Gaudet, K. Case, Linda Antonsson, Frauke Moebius, Jenny Graver, Noriko Shoji, Deborah Sumner, C. Joshua Villines, Mary Ellen Garland, Lauri M. Weaver, Christy Marx, Shauna Roberts, Catie Murphy, Ruth Stuart, Adrianne Middleton, Paula Mikkelsen, Paul "Princejvstin" Weimer, Pat Knuth, Mary Kay Kare, Peter Aronson, Rebecca Stefoff, Joseph Hoopman, Di, Valerie Nozick, M. Menzies, Nancy Pimentel, Dawn Marie Pares, Leah, Beth, SAMK, Anne Walker, April Steenburgh, Margaret C. Thomson, Ashley with the Morgans, M.L.K. Ondercin, Jaakko Kangasharju, Mary Spila, Poppy Arakelian, Sarah Patrick, Helen Wright, Paula Meengs, HY Tesler, Patricia Burroughs, Nancy Barber, Maryanne Stroud, Amanda Weinstein, K. Kisner, Pat Hayes, Kate Elliott, Phil Freund, Ceffyl, Solveig, Regina A. Tarr (hi, Mom!), Marti Wulfow Garner, Kerry Stubbs, Amy Sheldon, Mary Caelsto, Pat Cadigan, Christine Swendseid, Heidi Berthiaume, Sue Wolven, Donna P., Melinda Goodin from Australia, Kate Kirby, Cameron Harris, Ron Chance, Alison Farrin.

You are amazing. Thank you all.

# Dedication

For the real Meredith
who has waited very long and patiently
for her book to come out in the world

# Meredith

# Chapter 1

That was the absolute best and the absolute worst summer of my life, the summer I turned sixteen.

Sixteen is a weird year. Make it sixteen with your dad off finding himself again—not that he'd been around much even before the divorce—and your mom in remission from ovarian cancer, and you can pretty much figure you're being dumped on from somewhere.

What I didn't figure, and couldn't ever have figured, was how bad it was going to get—and how completely impossible both the bad and the good part would be.

Magic. It's dead, they say. Or never existed.

They aren't looking in the places I fell into, or finding it where I found it, that wonderful and terrible summer.

I had plans with the usual suspects: Cat and Rick and Kristen. They had their licenses already, got them before school let out. I was *this* close to mine, with the September birthday and being the class baby.

It was going to be our summer on wheels, when it wasn't on horseback or out on the beaches. We had it all mapped out.

Then Mom dropped the bomb.

I came home from the barn early that day, the day after the last day of school. Rick had the car, but his dad wanted it back by noon. So we'd hit the trails at sunup, then done our stalls and hay and water in a hurry with him already revving up the SUV.

When I got home, wringing wet and filthy and so smelly even I could tell I'd been around a manure pile, Mom was sitting out by the pool.

That wasn't where she usually was on a Thursday morning. She still had her work clothes on, but she'd tossed off the stodgy black pumps and splashed her feet in the water.

Her hair had all grown back since the chemo. It was short and curly, and still a little strange, but I liked it. I thought it made her look younger and prettier.

She turned and smiled at me. She looked tired, part of me said, but the rest of me told that part to shut up. "Good ride?" she asked.

"Good one," I answered. "Bonnie only threw in a couple of Airs. And that was because Rick was riding Stupid, and she was living up to her name. Bonnie had to put her in her place."

Mom laughed.

As long as I was out there, I figured I'd do the sensible thing. I dropped my shirt and riding tights and got down to the bathing suit any sane person wears under clothes in Florida summer, and dived into the pool.

The water felt absolutely wonderful. Mom watched me do a couple of laps.

Finally I gave in. I swam up beside her and folded my arms on the tiles and floated there, and said, "All right. Tell me."

She was still smiling. It must be something really good, to bring her out of court and all the way home.

"I've been talking to Aunt Jessie," she said. "She's staying in Egypt this summer, instead of coming back home to Massachusetts."

I knew that. I talked to Aunt Jessie, too. She Skyped in at least once a week. Checking on me, and on Mom through me.

But Mom was in story mode. I kept quiet and let her go on.

"She's really excited," Mom said. "She's made some discoveries that she thinks are very important, and with everything that's been going on over there, she hasn't been at all sure she can keep getting the permits. She actually got a grant, which is just about unheard of these days."

"She must be over the moon," I said.

"Oh, she is." Mom paused. "It's a big grant. Big enough for a whole team."

"Including you?"

That came out of the way Mom was smiling—excited, as if she had a secret and she couldn't wait to share. She'd been dreaming about Egypt for years, following all of Aunt Jessie's adventures and reading and studying and talking about maybe someday, if she had time, if she could get away, if—

There were always reasons not to go. First she had to make partner in the law firm. Then she got asked to be a judge in the county court, and that needed her to be always on. Always perfect. And then there was the cancer.

So maybe she figured it was now or never. I could see that. Even get behind it. But I wasn't sure how I felt about it.

Mom away for the whole summer? Was she really ready to leave me for that long? I didn't have my license yet. How was I going to—

All that zipped through my head between the time I asked my question and the time Mom answered, "Including you."

That stopped me cold.

Mom grinned at my expression. "You really thought it was me? I wish, but there are a couple of big cases coming on trial, and I might be called to the bench for another one, and—"

"You said you were going to take it easy this summer," I said. "We both were. What would I do in Egypt?"

"Learn," said Mom. "Explore. Be part of something big."

"Florida is big enough for me," I said. "What about Bonnie? And the trip to Disney World? And turtle watch? Turtle watch is important. The college needs us to count those eggs. That's big, too. It's real. It's now. Not fifty million years ago."

"Four thousand, give or take," said Mom, "and Disney World will keep. So will the turtles."

"Bonnie won't. Bonnie needs me. She just got bred. We don't even know if she's pregnant yet."

"We will tomorrow," Mom said. "You've got a week till you leave. It's all taken care of. Visas, everything. Aunt Jessie's been working on it for months. It's her birthday present to you."

She'd never said a word to me. Not even a hint.

"I hate surprises," I said. "I hate her."

"Hate me," Mom said. "It was my idea."

"It's your dream. Mine is to spend the summer with my friends and my horse. Not baking in a desert on the other side of the world. There are terrorists over there. Revolutionaries. Things get blown up. *People* get blown up."

"You will not get blown up," Mom said.

I pulled myself out of the water. "I'm not going," I said.

Mom didn't say anything. I grabbed a towel off the pile on the picnic table and rubbed myself dry, hard enough to make my skin sting, and marched off into the house.

For once in the history of the universe, none of the usual suspects was answering their phone. I barricaded myself in my room and went laptop surfing instead.

I surfed for horse stuff and beach stuff and turtle stuff. Nothing whatsoever to do with Egypt. Who cared about sand and terrorists and old dead mummies? The only sand I wanted was right underneath me in Florida.

When my phone whinnied at me, I almost didn't bother to answer it. After all, nobody could be bothered to answer me.

But the whinny was Cat, and she had an excuse. She'd been driving her kid brothers home from soccer.

*Crisis?* she texted.

Big time. But with the phone in my hand and the screen staring at me, I couldn't manage to fit it all into 160 characters. *Tell u tonight,* I said. *Still on for ice-cream run?*

*8:30,* she answered. *Rick too. Kelly's got a date.*

Normal me would have squeed and wanted to know all about it. Crisis me punched *OK. See u then,* and threw the phone on the bed.

Mom was still home. I could hear her rattling around in the kitchen. Then the TV came on, rumbling away in the background.

That was weird. I almost went to find out why she wasn't going back to work, but my mad was still too new. If she thought she was going to wait me out, she could just keep thinking it.

The computer beeped at me. The phone was lighting up with messages. *Now* everybody wanted to talk-text-email. All I felt like doing was crawling inside a book and pulling the cover over my head.

I tried every book in my to-be-read file, and even in my favorite-dead-tree-rereads pile, but my eyes kept slipping away from the words. Finally I opened my laptop instead, but I shut off the wi-fi.

It felt weird. Kind of guilty. Like telling the whole world to eff off.

What I needed was my own words, or words that came to me. Words that weren't about here or now. I needed to go away, really far away, deep inside myself where everything was different. Where I wasn't even me.

I've always told myself stories. I started writing them down as soon as I knew how. When I got my first computer that was all my own, I'd found the place where I could always go.

I wasn't always safe there. Stories aren't about being safe. On the screen, where the words were, I was home—more than I was anywhere except in the barn or in my own house.

A year ago, when the cancer came in, it was scary, but then there was the remission and I told myself that was it, we'd go on and nothing would change. Mom wouldn't get sick again.

But the world was different. I couldn't trust it any more.

The only world I could trust was the one I made for myself. The only light was on the screen, pale like moonlight, black like the sky between the stars. Outside it was a steaming hot Florida afternoon, with the sun beating down and the thunderheads piling up. In here, it was as cold as the truth I'd had to face, the day Mom came home from the doctor and sat me down and told me she was going to die.

Today wasn't anything like that. She was just dumping me for the summer—same as Dad used to do, till he stopped even bothering to show up. Just like Dad, she thought it was great. Romance! Adventure! All the things she'd never had time to do, so I got to do them instead.

I closed my eyes and made myself go away. Skip over. Ignore. Forget. Be somewhere else. Be someone else—someone as different as it was possible to be.

This wasn't really a new story. Pieces of it had been in me for as long as I could remember, fragments of words, images, half-remembered dreams, but now it was all there: solid, whole, and so real I could taste it.

Really, I could. It was bitter and salty, like a mouthful of ocean, or too many tears. When I opened my eyes, I was somewhere completely different.

I was inside the story. Instead of me telling it, it was telling me.

# Meru

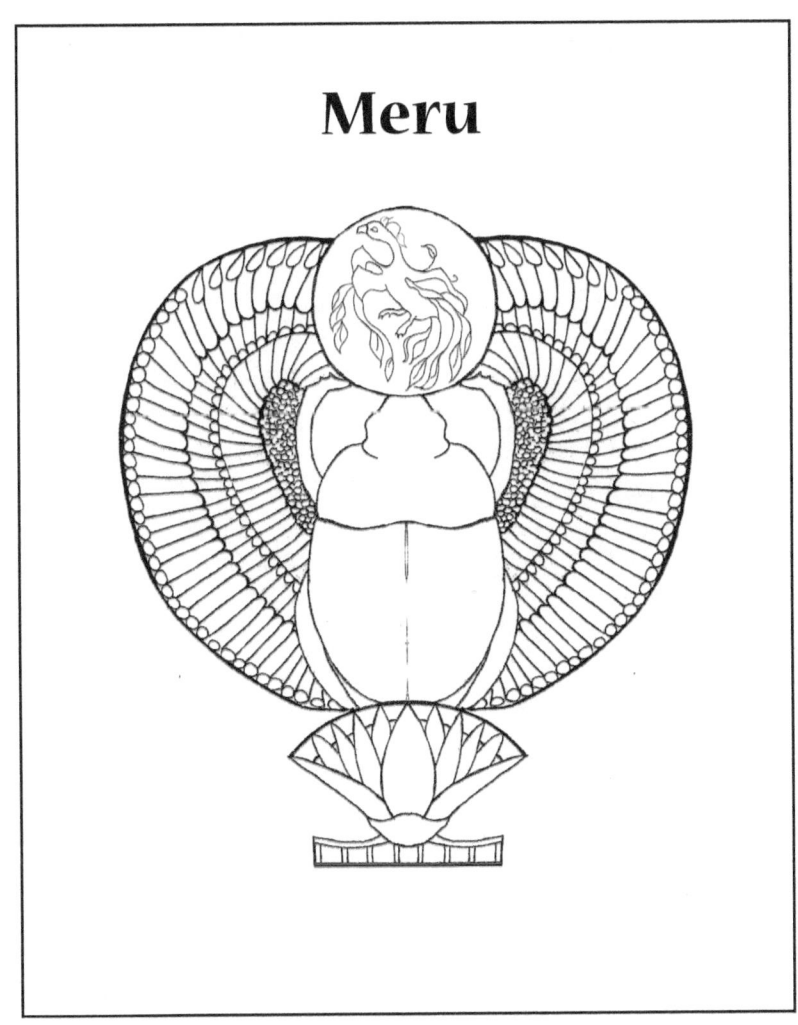

# Chapter 2

In all Meru's world, she was sure of two things: that she was born to be a starpilot, and that wherever her mother was, however far she wandered, she would always come home.

The message came over Earth's web one bitter-bright night, when the air outside the house was so cold it numbed the back of Meru's throat. She was the room she loved best in this world, high up in the family's house. Its ceiling was a force field, and by night it was transparent. When she slept there, she lay under the stars.

She had been sharing a webcircle with other star dreamers—Earthlings who dreamed of becoming starpilots. She and Yoshi, who had passed the tests and would be shipping out together to the starpilots' school, were basking in a cloud of joy and awe and envy.

It felt wonderful, and rather terrifying.

"This is how it will be for the rest of our lives," Yoshi said to her on an underchannel. "I don't know if I like it."

"We'll be ordinary enough at school," Meru said, "especially at the start, when everybody knows more than we do."

"Ai," said Yoshi. "You are right. I'm not sure I like that, either."

"It's worth it," she said.

His agreement hummed through the weblink.

The link broke abruptly. The message feed was corrupted, the words in it broken and blurred, but the priority tag was still on it, with the finder beacon that told Meru who had sent it.

Meru linked to the beacon and followed it, braced for a long search down the starways—and came to an abrupt and earthbound halt.

That should not have happened. She ran the search more times than she wanted to count, but the answer was always the same. Her mother, who should have been on the other side of the galactic sector, was on Earth, and close by. Something other than distance had garbled the message.

It could be an error, or a ghost in the web. Implants wore out. They could malfunction. There was no need to panic.

Yet.

"Meru? You there?"

The webcircle was still up, and still celebrating. Yoshi's ping was like a hot wire across bare skin.

"I'm here," she said.

"But what? What happened?"

"I can't talk. I can't stop. I have to go."

"Meru—"

She shut him off.

Her family gathered below, in the common room where everyone came together in the evenings, or curled in a warm and communal pile in one of the sleeping rooms. Meru missed the warmth suddenly, and the presence of all her cousins and the youngest aunts and uncles.

But two words in the stream had come through without static or garble. *Alone.*

And *Danger.*

Meru's mother was on Earth when she should have been exploring a distant system, and something was wrong.

The web offered no answers. Meru took a deep breath and made herself be calm. She searched for a new message, or even a slightly older one that might have told her more, but there was nothing about a woman of Earth named Jian, daughter and aunt of the family Banh-Liu, mother of Meru.

All Meru found was a babble of newsfeeds off the starweb. They were connected by a single key word: *Epidemic.*

There were always waves of disease on other worlds, plagues that came and went, infected aliens and unprotected humans, then ran their course and disappeared. They never reached Earth; the Consensus that governed it had such strong protections, and such effective quarantine and containment, that there had not been so much as a sniffle on the planet in a thousand years. Earth was the safest place there was, and Consensus had every intention of keeping it that way.

Jian must have been investigating a plague on one of the worlds she explored. Civilizations often rose and fell because of such things, and Jian would want to know everything: who and how and why, and whether the disease was still on the planet, waiting to break out again. It did not in any way explain why she was on Earth and sending such a weak and broken signal.

She could not be sick. If she were, Earth's protections would never have let her through.

That was not as reassuring as Meru would have liked it to be.

Over against the wall, a shadow stirred. Wings unfurled, half mist, half solid. Eyes glittered above a drift of fog that might have been a beak. The starwing stroked its half-substantial wingtip across Meru's cheek, a touch like ice and smoke, but strangely warm inside.

It always knew when she was sad or troubled—always had known, since her mother brought back the egg from one of her expeditions, and it hatched in Meru's hands. No one else she knew had a starwing. It was like a piece of the stars, to remind her of where she was going, and to keep her company when she went there.

She closed her eyes and let its presence soothe her. But not too much. She needed the sting of urgency.

She started down the lift to the common room, to the family and community and consensus. She would tell them what had come to her, and they would tell her what to do.

*Alone*, the message had said.

*Danger.*

Starpilots on voyage did not have community or consensus. They were alone with the ship and the stars. When danger threatened, they faced it— alone.

Meru sent the lift down the back way, away from the family.

She should have known it would not be that easy. No one was in the storage, but her cousin Ulani was in the kitchen, sitting under a lone, dazzling-bright light, finishing off the last of the pickled fish.

"You hate pickled fish," Meru said.

"I'm teaching myself to like it," Ulani said. She took a last bite, grimacing only slightly, and swallowed with an air almost of triumph.

"Ah," said Meru. "Because Aracele likes it."

Ulani's eyes dropped. Her feet shuffled. "I'm teaching her to like steamed buns. She says they taste like glue."

"They do," Meru said. "It really must be love, if you're both trying that hard to meet in the middle."

"She makes me warm inside," Ulani said. She looked as if she might have said more, but nothing came out.

Meru hugged her suddenly. "Go to bed. Dream about your sea-girl."

"Aren't you coming?" Ulani asked.

"In a while," Meru said.

She had to work hard to keep her voice from shaking. Ulani hesitated, as if she sensed something. Meru held her breath.

Ulani yawned. "Yes, I *am* tired. Don't you stay up too long, either."

"I'll try not to," Meru said.

Ulani was still yawning as she left the kitchen. Meru waited, listening hard. The whole family could decide to come down, and she would never get away at all.

The house was quiet. One or two of the aunts were on the house network, working through the night. Everyone else was either asleep or nearly there.

Meru gathered a few small things in a bag: a handful of protein bars, a bubble of water, one of the backups for her web implant. Her heart was beating, and she kept forgetting how to breathe.

*Foolish,* she said to herself. *In a pair of tendays you'll be going out alone into space, away from Earth, for a long time and maybe forever. This is only a little thing. A quick search. It's not even off the continent, let alone off the planet.*

When she scolded herself like that, she sounded like Grandmother Ramotswe. She could almost see the long finger shaking, and the dark eyes glaring the silliness out of her.

"I'll be back as soon as I find Jian," she said as if her grandmother had actually been there. "That is a promise." And she meant to keep it.

She left a ping on the data stream, a guide to where she had gone. The family would wake up to it in the morning. By that time or very soon after, Meru hoped, she would have found her mother, and be on her way back home.

She took a deep breath and stepped out of the house, into the breathtaking rush of the wind, and the roar of the sea.

The body suit she wore was a barely visible shimmer, but it was strong enough to protect her against the void of space. Earth's icy night was nothing to it. Meru allowed the air to penetrate to her face, gasping at the bite of it.

It was fierce, but it cleared her mind. She had been thinking of little past *Mother—urgent—wrongness—go.* Now she had a plan of sorts, and a trail to follow.

Hints and clues on the web led her from the house on its headland above the icy sea, down the empty road in the wind and the drifting snow. The starwing flew above her, shielding her with its wings. When she searched the web to find this road on this island, she saw no sign of herself, not even the flicker of a shadow.

The road down from the house was sand and stone, but it flowed into a smooth river of silver that looked somewhat like water and somewhat like ice. Meru paused before she stepped onto it. Once she set foot on that road, there would be no turning back.

She nearly did. A sleepy ripple on the web, a half-in-a-dream ping from her cousin Ti-shan, echoing and re-echoing through the streams of half a dozen other cousins and aunts and uncles, pulled at her with almost physical force. *Meru? What are you doing? You're not on the star-roads yet. Come down and share dreams with us.*

She wrenched away. Her mother needed her. She had to go.

She braced for the current that would seize her and carry her off the island. It caught her with startling gentleness and wrapped her in a bubble of warm air. Between one sharp-drawn breath and the next, she was skimming toward the dark bulk and distant brightness of the mainland.

No earthly thing could fly faster than the starwing. It flitted ahead and then back, circling above her, now blotting out the stars, now vanishing into them. The joy of its flight swelled inside her. It was almost enough to dim the anxiety and fear that had brought her out on this bitter night.

Jian's track through the web was fading, but Meru had found the source, mapped and marked it. She only had to get there, and try not to think too hard on what she would find.

The old city sprawled under and around the spaceport. Even in daylight, most of it lay in shadow: the long ribbon of the starcable blocked the sun, unwinding toward the station and the starships that hovered above the atmosphere. Cars ran and up and down it like beads of light on an endless string.

Once the road touched the mainland, traffic flowed into it: drone transports mostly at this hour, carrying cargo to the port. Meru in her bubble was the only single human, though she saw a handful of others traveling in twos and threes.

The starwing had vanished overhead, but it was still there, watching over Meru. She found that comforting. This was far from the first time she had come to the port. But she had never come alone before, and never at night.

She could not afford to be afraid. She focused all of herself on the moment when the road ended and she had to walk.

Properly brought up people never went to the old city. It was a wild place, and dangerous. There were creatures in there who had no link to the web; humans, even, whose implants had failed, or who had never been implanted at all.

Without the web, there was no Consensus. Meru tried to imagine a mind that could not, at the spark of a neuron, reach out to the whole universe of information. What must it be like to be completely and permanently alone?

Now as she hunted the last fading fragments of her mother's message, she wondered, with a shiver of horror, if Jian had lost or destroyed her implant.

Jian would never do that. She loved to soar through the web, to link to the webs of other worlds and explore their strangeness, just as she loved to explore the physical reality of earth and stone and sky. Jian was complete in everything she was, mind and body.

Meru shut down the rest of the thought before she disintegrated into panic. The road's end loomed ahead of her: a cluster of domes and arches with the lighted column of the cable rising beyond them. She focused firmly on it.

Her bubble popped with a rush of frigid air and deposited her on the solid steady surface of the platform. The drones rumbled and purred onward through the tunnel to the port. The humans followed on a lesser road, skimming more slowly but just as irresistibly toward light and safety.

There was nothing in the port for Meru. She turned away from the light toward flickering dimness.

This corridor had no ribbon of road to carry her. It was low and narrow and dingy and old. It smelled like bare ground under snow, and like the ghosts of ancient chemicals: sulfur, benzene, and a distant bite of hydrochloric acid.

Mist and warmth enfolded her. The starwing had come down out of the sky. It shrank until it was hardly larger than its youngest hatchling self, and wrapped its half-solid, half-insubstantial body around her neck and shoulders.

It had no weight, but it had presence. It purred softly in her ear.

It gave her courage. When the lights in the passage grew so dim she could barely see, it cast a glow ahead of her, faint but clear. She stroked the edge of its wing in gratitude.

The corridor ended in a platform only a little like the one at road's end. No road waited there to carry her onward. Instead there was a wall, with the shimmer of a force field around and above it.

There were gates in the wall. When she called up their schematic on the web, it marked them as guarded, but the watch systems were as tired and faded as the rest of the old city. She convinced the one nearest to see nothing but a gust of wind as she passed by.

After she had done that, she stopped. Why had she done that? There was no need to hide. The aunts and uncles would rebuke her for going so far alone, but they could hardly stop her now.

Her mother's signal was nearly gone. So was any time Meru might have had to waste. She had too much sense to attract notice by running, but she walked quickly through the gate.

The city was a maze. Dark walls rose above her. Things moved in the shadows. In what light there was, people crowded together, talking, laughing, singing.

Meru had not expected the singing. Or the music, either, that boomed or jangled or lilted out of every window and door. It should have been a deafening noise, but it all flowed together somehow, like the countless data streams of the web.

She had never been in a crowd of live and breathing people before. Bodies jostled her, crowding her forward.

The starwing hissed. The large figure that had been caroming toward her veered sharply off. She had sense enough to keep moving, and to try to avoid colliding with anyone.

On the web it was different. People did not crash into each other there, with bruises to show for it. Or step on toes. Or yell in her face, blowing warm rank breath over her, and saying things that made her cheeks go hot and her ears burn.

It was like swimming in the rocks along the island's edge, pushed and pulled by the ocean's currents. Once Meru understood that, the movement of the crowd began to make sense. Then she could dart and swerve and sidestep in much the same dance as the rest.

While she concentrated on getting through the crush of people, she almost let go of the map and the beacon. In a surge of panic, she ran another link to them.

Not so far now. It would have been easier if she had dared to close her eyes. She had to try to navigate both the street with its noise and crowds, and the web that kept promising an easy and simple way to the spark that said, *Here. She was here.*

There was nothing simple about the old city. The map must have been nearly as old: not all the streets led as it directed. Gaps and rubble lay where the map marked buildings, and streets ended abruptly or took unexpected turns.

The starwing unfurled from Meru's neck and flew upward. Under the surge and flow of the web in Meru's mind was something like a thought and something like an image of the starwing rising above the tops of the buildings, mapping what was there and matching it to the map on the web. And then, at the end, the starwing's search found warmth and a faint scent of alien flowers that said *Jian.*

Part of Meru wanted desperately to cling to the starwing, but she needed its view of the city from above. She stumbled into a doorway, pressed into a corner that stank of cats and something rank that was not, somehow, earthly, and squeezed her eyes shut.

*There.*

The starwing had found the last bits of broken data that belonged to Meru's mother.

They were in the oldest of the old sector, which was half in ruins; half of the rest was overgrown with stark and winter-withered trees. The wall around it was newer but still ages old, its force field patched and re-patched, but still full of gaps.

On the far side, nearest the port, the wall had begun to mend. The strength of the field fed the starwing like a blaze of sunlight, making it so giddy that it spun upward toward the stars.

Meru's cry brought it back. It hovered above the place where Jian had been, where Meru hoped desperately that she still was.

Meru had to move quickly. The field was spreading to close off the sector.

She knew that because the starwing knew it. There was nothing about that field on the web, no warning or explanation—and that was strange.

She took as deep a breath as she could bear to, sighted along the crowd and sprang into it, aiming as best she could toward the place where the starwing waited.

# Meredith

# Chapter 3

I snapped awake, and caught my laptop before it slid off my lap to the floor. My neck had a kink in it. I eeped when I tried to unkink it.

I'd been asleep sitting up. My story was still on the screen, the one I'd been writing before I fell into that dream or hallucination or whatever it was. It had nothing whatsoever to do with a girl named Meru or a world of ice and darkness or a creature called a starwing.

That was the weirdest dream I had ever had. Weirder still, I could remember every detail of it.

I don't remember dreams, not like that. But this one wouldn't let go. If I closed my eyes, I could see the half-broken city, and hear it and feel it and smell it.

Especially smell it. I know what the projects smell like, and there was plenty of that, but there were other things, things I couldn't put a name to. Alien things. Weird and sharp, catching at the throat; making my eyes water.

I was freaking myself out. I snapped the laptop shut a little harder than I really needed to, though the dream didn't have anything to do with it at all, and pushed it away.

While I'd been dreaming my science-fiction dream, the sun had gone down. Mom was asleep on the couch—I freaked again till I made sure she was breathing. Then I told myself she didn't look sick. Of course not. Just tired.

I was still mad at her. That hadn't changed a bit.

Dinner hadn't made itself while both of us slept. I found the rest of the roast chicken from yesterday and made a salad out of it, but when I went to wake Mom up, I couldn't face another round of Yes You're Going, No I'm Not. I let her sleep.

I wasn't hungry anyway. I covered the bowl and shoved it in the fridge, and left Mom a note on the board: *Salad in fridge. Gone to Ice Creamery with Cat and Rick.*

"Seriously?" said Cat. "They're giving you *Egypt* for your birthday?"

When Cat gets excited she gets squeaky. She was up in bat territory now.

Between that and the arctic air conditioning and the solar-flare lighting, the Ice Creamery was a migraine waiting to happen. I'd had a psycho break and ordered a Bama Slammer, which was a double banana split with blackberries, pecans, peaches, three different sauces, and enough ice cream to feed a third-world country.

I already had brain freeze from eating the first few spoonfuls too fast. I picked at the rest while Cat gnawed on her Choco-Cone. In between bites she kept squeaking. "*Egypt*! King Tut! Pyramids! Barging down the Nile!"

"Terrorists," I said, two solid octaves down from her. "Sandstorms. Mummies."

"Mummies are fascinating," Rick said. He wasn't really paying attention: he had his tablet and the game of Mighty World of Gruesome Gory War he was playing with his friend-if-you-know-what-I-mean, Greg from space camp at the Cape. Between that and his Authentic New York City Egg Cream, he was as happy as he could get when he wasn't on a horse.

"Mummies are gruesome," Cat said. "Mummies are wonderful. Will you be digging up any?"

"No," I said. "I'm not going."

"That's crazy," Cat said. "Of course you're going. It's the trip of a lifetime. You have to go."

"My mom's lifetime," I said, "and I *don't* have to. I want to stay here." My Bama Slammer had started to melt into a pool of purple and orange and off-white. I stirred it together into purple-tinged mud. It was about the color of Cat's hair.

"They have horses in Egypt," Rick pointed out. He turned his tablet so I could see.

There was a lot of sand. A Pyramid. And a rider in a helmet on a delicate little horse.

*Giza Adventure Tours,* the caption said. *See the Pyramids the Old-Fashioned Way.*

I pushed the tablet back at Rick. "That's up near Cairo," I said. "I'd be stuck a thousand miles away, digging around in old tombs."

"There must be horses there, too," he said. "Or camels. I always wanted to ride a camel."

"I did once," Cat said. "When Dad was stationed in Saudi. It's like the most back-breaking Warmblood trot you ever sat. I almost got whiplash."

"Lovely," I said.

Cat popped the last of the Choco-Cone into her mouth and crunched it into submission. She'd flipped out of squee mode into frowny-serious. "All I got for my sixteenth was a fourth-hand minivan. You get a whole country."

"I'd rather have the minivan," I said.

She threw her scrunched-up napkin at me. It caught me dead between the eyes.

I threw it back—three feet off target. "Why didn't *you* go to Egypt? You were right there."

"Dad got sent to Afghanistan. The rest of us came over here."

I knew that. I was being a jerk, but I couldn't seem to stop. "You and Mom can go. I'll stay here."

"I wish." Cat pushed herself away from the noisy little table.

She was pissed off at me. I didn't blame her, but I wasn't going to apologize, either. She was my friend. She was supposed to be on my side.

Rick wasn't any help. He was winning his stupid game with his stupid friend. That was all he cared about.

We didn't say much in the car on the way home. When Cat dropped me off, she kept on giving me the silent treatment. Rick's half-absent voice floated out the back window of the minivan. "See you at the barn."

"I'll be there early," I said.

"Crack of dawn," said Rick as Cat gunned the minivan down the street.

Mom was in bed when I got in. Good. I didn't have to talk to her.

I should go to bed, too: when I'd said I'd be at the barn early, I hadn't been kidding. Six a.m. for feeding and stalls. Then ride. Then, vet emergencies willing, Bonnie's preg check.

I was too restless and pissy and sugar-shocky to sleep. My laptop was open; when I woke it up, the story I'd been poking at was still there.

I halfway expected it to mutate into another science-fiction dream, but I wasn't likely to have one of those again. I was a little sorry. I would have liked to know what had happened to Meru's mom, and why the old city was being cordoned off, and...

Maybe I'd write my way through the rest of it. But not tonight.

I went to put my laptop on the bedside table, and found something in the way. A book.

It used to live on the coffee table in our old house, when I was little and Dad was still more often there than not. It was my favorite book in the whole world.

I cussed out Mom for thinking she could get me that way. When I reached for the book, meaning to throw it in the general direction of the closet, I found myself pulling it into my lap instead.

It fell open to the chapter xon the Valley of the Kings. I used to imagine myself standing on that red sand, looking across the desert to the blue, blue sky. The green country—the Black Land, the old Egyptians called it, because the soil was so rich and dark—was behind me. I could feel the harsh dry heat and smell the sharp dry smell that hadn't changed in five thousand years.

A wave of sleep hit me so hard I almost fell over. I left the book where it was and dropped into bed.

I understood something then, just on the edge of sleep, but when I woke up, I couldn't remember. All I took with me was the memory of the sand and the sun, and a voice saying words in a language I couldn't understand.

Except that, somehow, I could. *It's all one,* the voice said.

I had no idea what it meant. And I didn't care. I just knew it was right.

# Meritre

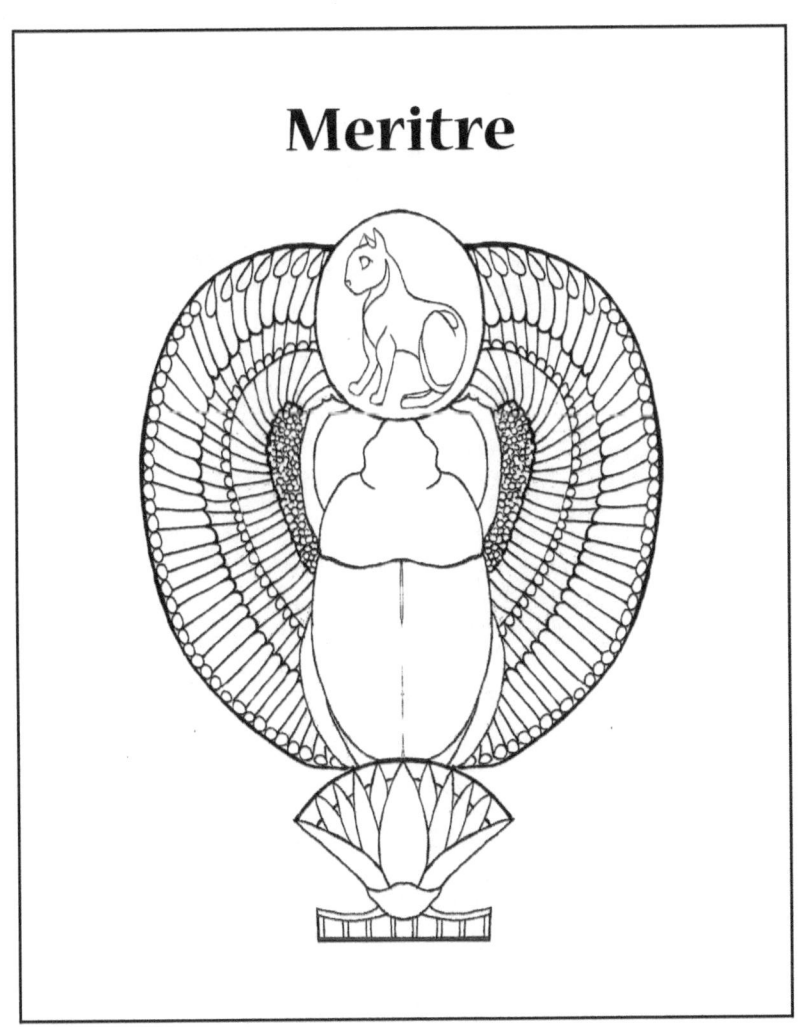

# Chapter 4

A hawk hung on the pinnacle of heaven. From the temple far below, it looked like a bird of metal suspended in the sky.

The sun's heat was fierce, but Meritre shivered. The choir was so much smaller than it had been a year ago: so many lost, so many voices silenced. Of those whom the plague had left, too many were thin and pale, and their singing barely rippled the air above the courtyard.

They would be strong again. New voices would join the chorus. Pharaoh had promised, swearing that the promise came from the great god Amon himself.

Today, there were only twelve singers, and somehow they had to sing as if there were three times that many. The plague was gone at last. In just nine days there would be a royal rite of celebration, and the choir would sing the responses.

The mistress of the chorus struck the stone paving with her rod. "Again," she said. "Clearer, louder, stronger. The king will be here, and the king's daughter. Give them a hymn worthy of the god himself."

Meritre filled her heart and head and throat with the song and poured it out with all the strength she had. Eleven voices joined with hers, swelling until they filled the great court with its brilliantly painted columns and its ranks of statues both royal and divine. Even the blue vault of heaven and the hawk of Horus hovering in it seemed to pause, struck motionless by the sound.

One voice faltered, lost its power and swiftly died. It was the one of them all that Meritre knew best, the purest and until now the strongest.

She turned in time to see her mother fall. The singers on either side leaped to catch her, but Meritre was there first. Her knees were bruised from the pavement; her mother was a dead weight in her arms.

Aweret still breathed, though shallowly. Her skin was damp and unnaturally cold.

The plague came with a cough and a burning fever. These chills must be something else, something less deadly—from the heat, maybe. It was terribly hot in the courtyard, and they had been rehearsing since the early morning. It was a miracle that no one else had fainted.

One of the temple servants brought a cup full of barley water. Meritre held it to her mother's lips. Aweret drank a sip or two, then turned her head away.

The mistress of the chorus was a sharp and irritable woman, but her heart was kind. She insisted on sending Aweret home in a chair like one of the priests. Aweret was weak enough not to object—and that frightened Meritre all over again.

She held herself together well enough to make her way home, though she hardly remembered the streets between. Those were much less crowded than they used to be, and the markets were almost empty.

The servants from the temple helped her carry Aweret up to the roof where there was a fan and a shade and as much coolness as anyone could find in this season. No one else was in the house. Father and the boys were in the king's workshop, carving statues as they did every day except festival days.

Meritre dampened the shade in the jar of water that she always kept filled, and hung it up to catch the wind. It cooled the air where Aweret lay. She sighed, and Meritre thought she looked a little less pale.

The cat who had chosen to live in this house came gliding out of air as cats could do. It sprang up onto the cot and curled in the curve of Aweret's hip.

Aweret was well guarded now. Meritre wanted to stay beside her, too, but there was too much to do: bread to bake, beer to brew, dinner to get ready for the others when they came home in the evening. She stooped to kiss Aweret's forehead and smooth her hair.

Aweret's eyes were open, and they were clear. Meritre never meant to burst into tears.

Aweret caught Meritre's hand before she could spin away, and said, "I'm well. I'm not sick or dying."

"Then what?" Meritre tried, but she could not keep the anger out of her voice. "You scared half my souls out of me."

"I am sorry," Aweret said. "I wasn't sure, you see, and I didn't want to tell anyone, even your father, for fear it wouldn't be true. But while we were singing, while the rays of the god were bathing my face, I knew. I'm afraid it overwhelmed me."

"You *are* sick," Meritre said, "or the sun has driven you insane."

"Oh, no," Aweret said, laughing. "Here. It's here." She laid Meritre's hand on her middle, where it was always gently rounded, but maybe, now, just a little more.

Meritre stared. Aweret nodded. Her eyes were full of joy. "It's an omen," she said. "The terrible times truly are gone. This child brings blessing to us all."

"Gods willing," Meritre said.

She was glad—really, she was. But more than that, she was terrified.

The plague had been kind to her family. It had only killed the baby, little Iry; it had left the rest of them alone.

Babies were so fragile. Any smallest thing could sweep them away. That had been true of every human life in the plague, but a new one, so young it had just begun to wake to the world, was most vulnerable of all.

Meritre did not know if she dared to love another sister or brother as she had loved Iry. A part of her had gone away when her sister died, and still had not come back.

She set another kiss on her mother's belly where her hand had been. A thought was growing in her, but she needed time to let it take root. "You rest," she said. "The others will be home soon. I won't tell them. Unless...?"

Aweret laid a finger on Meritre's lips. "It will be our secret for a while."

"Not too long," Meritre said.

"Oh, no," said Aweret. "Even a man will notice eventually—and your father has a sharper eye than most."

"That's the sculptor in him," Meritre said. She claimed back her hand and made herself stand up straight. "Now I really have to go, or dinner will be late, and they'll all ask too many questions."

Aweret's secret was heavy inside Meritre, as if she had a baby in her, too, but one made of stone. While her mother slept on the other side of the roof,

Meritre retreated behind the screen to the kitchen. She ground the barley into flour, made the bread and stirred up the stew of lentils and onions and salt fish. It was familiar work, and welcome, but her mind kept on spinning through it.

Just after the bread was done, she heard the commotion coming down the street, a boisterous male noise that made her smile in spite of herself.

The smile died. One of them was coughing. The deep, hacking sound brought back every memory and every nightmare of the plague: people coughing up blood, their faces turning black, their eyes rolling up in their heads as they wheezed and gagged and died.

Meritre staggered and almost fell into the cooking fire. Sheer stubbornness saved her. She would *not* faint. There had been enough of that today.

Her brothers tumbled up onto the roof, with her father bringing up the rear. He was still coughing, but not so hard now.

"Stone dust," he said when Meritre leaped toward him. She must have looked as panicked as she felt: he hugged her tight and kissed her, and stroked her as if she had been the cat. "There now. We've started the new statue, and the dust has been worse than usual. A jar or two of beer and I'll be as good as new."

She wanted to believe it. She needed to. She brought him his beer and tried not to hover while he drank it.

The boys were starving, loudly. While she fed them, she could stop thinking about her mother having a baby and her father coming home with a cough.

It was going to be well. The plague had taken all the lives it meant to take. Meritre promised herself that.

Whatever she had to do to make it so, she would do. She promised that, too, deep in her heart, where only the gods could hear.

# Meredith

# Chapter 5

The sun wasn't even up when Kristen pulled into the driveway. I was ready and waiting for her, with my head still full of heat and sand and somebody else's gut-grinding worry.

That was the second dream I'd ever had that I not only hadn't forgotten, I couldn't get it out of my head. It made more sense, sort of. I'd gone to sleep with the Valley of the Kings in my head. But the whole thing was weird.

Too weird for that hour of the morning. I almost forgot my phone—had to run back in and get it—but Kristen was too full of last night's date to mind.

She started talking as soon as I got the door shut and the seat belt fastened. Devon this and Devon that and Devon everything else.

I never had got around to asking Cat who Kristen's date was. Finally I got a word in sideways. "Devon? Devon Mackey?"

She came down to earth for a second. "Of course Devon Mackey. Who did you think it was?"

I hadn't been thinking at all. At least not about that.

"I know he's captain of the wrestling team," Kristen said. "He can't help it if he's built like that, really, can he? He's got it. He might as well use it. He's thinking about applying to M.I.T. His dad wants him to go to Stanford, but he likes Boston. Besides, can you imagine? A wrestling scholarship to M.I.T. Heads will explode."

My head was thinking about exploding, but not because of Devon Mackey, wrestling star and future rocket scientist.

Kristen kept on talking about the amazing, incredible, fantastic Devon and the fantastic, incredible, amazing date. I sneaked a look at my phone. *You Have No New Messages.*

Well, not on the phone. In my head...

Two dreams so real they were like living two whole new and completely different lives, worrying about mothers. I got it. I did.

I sucked it up enough to pop off a text to my mom. *Vet @930. Don't forget.*

I didn't expect an answer. Didn't get one.

With Kristen's voice rising and falling in my ear, I watched the road unroll. Mom and I lived on a narrow sandspit between the ocean and the river. Kristen turned off it onto the causeway, up and over and into the sand and the palmettos and the long empty roads that the developers hadn't raped and pillaged yet.

Mangrove Farm used to be out in the middle of nowhere, but an RV park and a Seven-Eleven had popped up at the intersection, and there was a sign threatening a new condo development. *COMING SOON!* it screamed.

It had been screaming at us for the past three years. Maybe we'd get lucky and *soon* would never come at all.

Kristen shut up when we left the pavement and got onto the dirt road. You had to pay attention to where the ruts were to keep from bouncing off into the palmettos.

"It helps to drive a little bit fast," I said. "Skim the ruts."

"Thank you for your expert advice," Kristen said through clenched teeth. Her knuckles were white where she gripped the steering wheel.

My phone whinnied. Text from Mom.

*Honey, I'm sorry. I got called in to work. The lawyers want to settle, and the meeting is at 9. I'll come as soon after that as I can. Give Bonnie a smooch from me.*

Speaking of *soon,* and never happening. Maybe the vet would never show up, either. Maybe Bonnie wasn't pregnant at all.

The car lurched. Kristen swore. She almost overshot the farm gate, but swerved just in time.

After that much adventure, poop-scooping was restful. Hardly anybody was there yet, but Cat came stumbling in while I was halfway through my third stall. She had a serious case of bed head, half of the short spiky neopunk crop standing straight up and half mashed flat. She'd touched up the purple: it was the exact shade I get when I leave the bluing in Bonnie's mane too long after a bath.

Rick was already out in the arena, schooling over jumps before the heat came up. I stopped to watch him clear an in-and-out, collect into a beautiful almost-pirouette, and aim at the Wall of Death, which was set at five feet. For Rick that was just a pop-over.

Rick's not my type and I'm definitely not his, but Rick on a horse is a thing of beauty. He's a middle-sized guy, mostly legs—on foot he's kind of ordinary, you know, brown floppy hair, geek glasses. But get him in a saddle and you can't tell where the horse starts and he leaves off.

I stopped to give him the admiration he deserved, and to crunch down on the jealous part. You'd never catch me dead jumping five feet, let alone six. I'd probably *be* dead if I tried.

It was all perfectly peaceful and ordinary. The part that wasn't was me holding off on visiting Bonnie in the pasture. I could see her out there, a stocky white shape in the middle of all the big leggy brown ones.

She could see me, too, but she was busy being queen. Bonnie ruled the mare pasture with an iron hoof.

Bonnie's registered name is Bonamia. Most people think she's some kind of fat white pony, because she's short and she's built like a brick and she's got serious—I mean serious—opinions about how the world is supposed to work.

Then she moves, and you know there's something more going on. Bonnie in motion is pure magic. Then you can see she was born to dance in front of kings.

Bonnie is a Lipizzaner. Yes, real people can own one of those. Lipizzaners are really rare, though not nearly as expensive as you might think, and it was our duty to posterity, Mom said, to make sure Bonnie made another one. It was Mom's idea to do it this year. She'd let me pick the stallion, but she drew up the list I picked him from.

This was supposed to be our family project. She hadn't been there for the breeding, either—vet, turkey baster, boy-in-a-box shipped all the way from Arizona. Work again.

Egypt I was mad about. This just made me tired.

I finished my stalls, and Cat and I got the water buckets filled. By then Kristen had started her dressage lesson and Rick was on to jump school number two. Her blonde ponytail and his screaming-flames helmet took turns bobbing around the dressage and jumping rings.

It was almost time for the vet—though vet time is like Dad time: it takes as long as it takes.

Cat went down with me to the pasture. Her big bay mare was Bonnie's BFF; the two of them were waiting at the gate when we got there, with the rest of the ladies-in-waiting hanging back respectfully and the south-pasture geldings keeping a wary distance. Nobody messed with Bonnie and Dora.

As soon as I saw my fat white pony, I forgot everything else but her. I wasn't making any hopes or plans yet, but she looked even whiter and shinier than usual. There was a glow on her.

She pushed her nose into the halter and I buckled it, and then stood for a long time with my face in her mane, breathing the smell of clean horse. She didn't pull away as quickly as she usually did. I thanked her for that when I finally stepped back and took a deep breath and looked up to see the vet's truck pulling in by the nearer barn.

I could say I felt something building around me. I could say Bonnie farts rainbows, too. I wasn't feeling anything right then but annoyance with Mom and excitement about the vet.

Bonnie danced a little on the way up from the pasture to the wash rack, as if she knew something big was about to happen. Dr. Kay was waiting for us with her laptop that was, among other things, an ultrasound machine. She smiled at me and said to Bonnie, "Well, your majesty. Ready to show us what you've got in there?"

Bonnie snorted and pulled ahead of me toward the wash rack. Cat laughed behind me. Maybe Dora did, too. "She knows," Cat said.

"Now the rest of us get to find out," said Dr. Kay.

I led Bonnie into the wash rack, which did double duty as a breeding stanchion. Dr. Kay fastened the butt bar and plugged in the ultrasound probe.

Bonnie knew the drill from her breeding exams and her date with the boy-in-a-box. She didn't exactly like it—would *you* like having somebody's arm shoved all the way up where the sun don't shine? But she'd been on board with this from the start, and she wasn't changing her mind now.

Bonnie is a whole lot smarter than your average horse. On her end of the horse-brains scale, weird is perfectly normal.

I had Bonnie's leadrope to manage, but while Dr. Kay probed and stretched and peered at the laptop screen, I angled around till I could get a glimpse of Bonnie's grainy, blurry insides.

The image stopped shifting and turning and zeroed in. There was something in the middle: a perfect black circle with a white dot at the top.

Dr. Kay lit up with a grin. "There's your baby," she said.

I burst into tears. It was totally embarrassing, and of course the whole world was there, from Barb the barn owner to Kristen with her Warmblood and Rick with big red Stupid, and Cat and Dora looking as if they'd put on the whole show. The humans were all grinning and clapping and cheering and kindly not noticing that my eyes were running over.

Bonnie got cookies and carrots and a proud pat from Dr. Kay. Nobody said anything about the person who wasn't there—who should have been. I aimed my phone at the ultrasound screen, which Dr. Kay had frozen and saved, and sent the picture to Mom.

She'd get it when she got it. I told myself I didn't care.

It was Cat who asked the question I couldn't get it together to ask. "So now what? Anything special we should do?"

"Not much," Dr. Kay answered. "Keep on riding and exercising her, and don't change her feed for now. We'll check her again in a month, make sure everything's where it belongs. Then it's hurry up and wait."

"345 days, give or take," I said. "Only 330 to go."

"Give or take," said Dr. Kay. She gave Bonnie one last pat and me one last smile, and packed up and drove off to her next appointment.

Lunch was also our weekly Skype with Aunt Jessie—live from beautiful Luxor, as she liked to put it. The only reason I even did it was because Mom trapped me.

Mom showed up at the barn just before I was about to take off with Cat and Kristen. I couldn't very well not show her the rest of the ultrasound pictures, or refuse to let her love on Bonnie and tell her what a wonderful, amazing, miraculous horse she was.

Then Mom said handed me the car keys and said, "You're driving home."

Bribery works. Cat grinned at me. "See you tonight," she said.

"Turtle time," I agreed.

Mom didn't gloat. That wasn't how she operated. She kissed Bonnie's nose and fed her the last carrot in the bag.

I had the car started and the A/C blasting by the time she tore herself away from Bonnie. "When I grow up," I said, "I'm moving to Iceland."

"Not Antarctica?"

"No horses."

"Point," she said, strapping herself in.

I drove carefully, minding my driver's education manual. I swear the road got rougher every time I went down it.

Mom was quiet. Dozing, I noticed. She did a lot of that these days.

I thought about slowing down even more, but my back teeth were already rattling out of my head. Mom only flinched at the worst of the bumps. By the time we reached the blissful smoothness of the paved road, she was sound asleep.

I'd exhausted my worry quota months ago. I told myself she was doing this to wear me down till I gave in about Egypt. I really couldn't go now, could I? Dr. Kay was coming back in a month. Somebody had to be there for that.

We had lunch with Aunt Jessie—virtually. It was dinnertime over there. We put my laptop at her usual place at the table and ate our ham and cheese while she ate her chicken and veg.

I didn't have much to say. Mom was all full of Bonnie and the ultrasound and the baby.

Finally she stopped pushing it and picked at her sandwich, which she'd eaten a whole quarter of. Aunt Jessie in Luxor was mopping the bottom of her bowl with a chunk of bread.

I peeled my dessert orange piece by piece.

"All right," Aunt Jessie said to me. "So that didn't go well, did it? Still hate surprises?"

"Hate," I said to the pile of orange peel. "Not coming. I'm sorry."

"No, you're not sorry," she said, "and yes, you're coming. Check your email. There's a shopping list. You're good on shots—while you're getting your hate on, hate Dr. Meldrum, he gave you one or two last month that weren't on the school list for fall."

That didn't surprise me at all. "Is that even legal?"

"Minor child," Aunt Jessie said with complete lack of remorse. "Parental discretion. It's for your own good. Once you get here, you'll love it. Or I'll be working you so hard you won't have time to hate it."

"What if I just won't get on the plane? I'll show up with a gallon of hair gel and a riding whip. Raise a stink in the naked scanner."

"Get arrested. End up on a terrorist watch list. Get hauled off to juvie. Is that what you still call it?" Aunt Jessie grinned. Even through the blurry, jerky screen I could see how much fun she was having. "As long as you're going to spend your summer in durance vile, you might as well spend it here. The food is better and the doors unlock from the inside."

"You'd better hope I don't spend my time learning ancient Egyptian curses. I'll put one on you."

"I'll curse you back," she said cheerfully. "And I've had 'way more practice. See you next Friday. I'll meet you at the airport."

She shut the call down from her end. I stared at the empty screen. My own face reflected back at me. I put a mental caption on it. *POWERLESSNESS: It's What's for Lunch.*

"It's just for six weeks," Mom said. "You'll still have a month to spend with your friends before school starts."

"But not with Bonnie."

"Bonnie will be perfectly fine. I'll check in on her. You know your friends will. *You* can check in on her from online. She'll be the most checked-in-on horse on the eastern seaboard."

She was being reasonable. I didn't want to be reasonable. I wanted to pitch a roaring fit.

A year ago I might have done it. Too bad I had to grow up enough to have some impulse control.

I cleared the table instead, and tossed the leftovers in the disposal and the dishes in the dishwasher.

"We'll go shopping tomorrow," said Mom.

"Do I get to pick my own prison uniform?"

"As long as it's on the list."

"Pith helmet? Sword cane?"

"Possibly even goggles," she said, "and a white silk scarf."

That was our old joke. When I was little, we were going to fly around the world in a biplane, and spy on Dad wherever he happened to be that week.

"Dad's not in Egypt," I said. "Is he?"

"Not that I know of." Mom stood up and stretched. "I have a little work to do still. Then we'll go out for dinner. Celebrate Bonnie's baby."

I opened my mouth to say no thanks, I wasn't celebrating anything today. Damn impulse control. What came out was, "Fine. Whatever."

Mom kissed me the way she did when I was six, a flying swoop on the forehead, and went off to do her judge thing. I had the house to myself and an afternoon to kill, and a few people to contemplate killing.

So I did what any self-respecting writer type does. I holed up with my laptop and killed off a bunch of characters. Bloodily. With lots of screaming.

# Meru

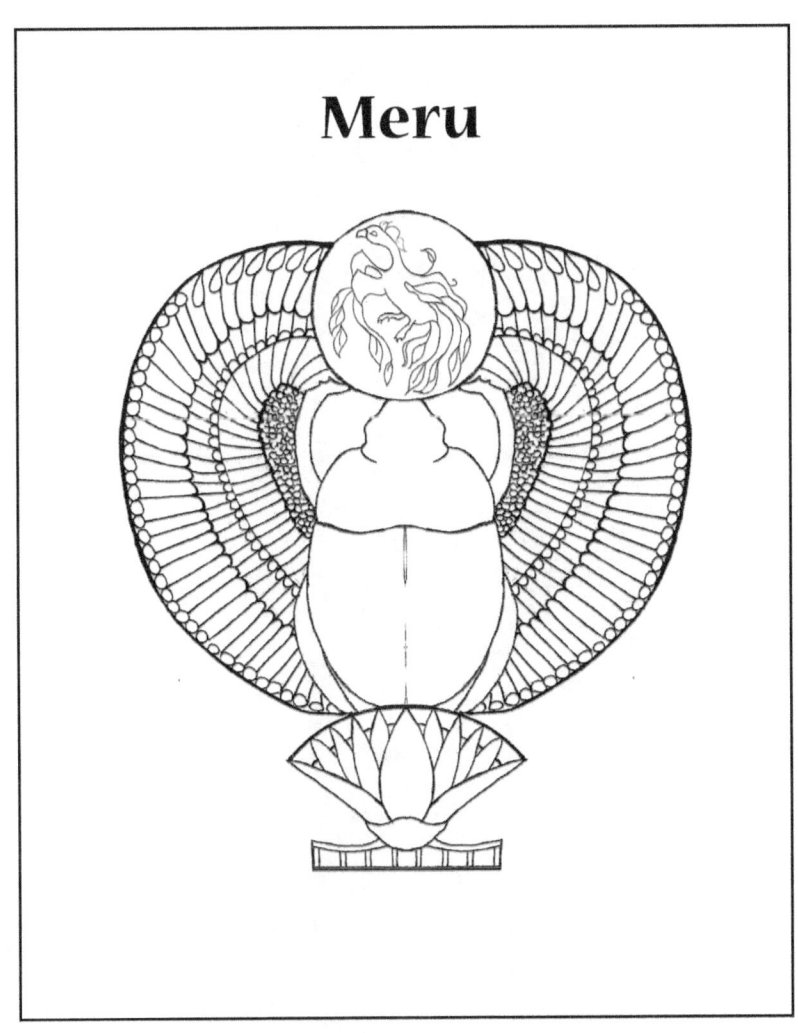

# Chapter 6

The gaps in the force field were closing. The oldest sector of the old city was almost out of reach. Meru fought her way through crowds so thick they seemed to have been put there deliberately to stop her. That was impossible. The web was the same as ever, no mention of anything in the old city, though Meru ran search after search while she struggled to get to the oldest sector before the field walled it off completely.

Up above them all, the starwing circled slowly, invisible against the darkness and the starlight. As Meru's desperation mounted, it began to feed on the field.

This time it fed slowly. It skimmed the edges of the surging energy, drawing off just enough to slow the field's advance.

Meru reached the wall just ahead of the hum and flicker of the field—a handful of nanoseconds before it closed. She dived through the broken gate, tripped and fell and lay winded in a street as empty as the one outside had been full of people.

There had to be people here. The web said there were, and the starwing could see and feel them, sparks of warmth inside the cold walls of brick and steel and stone.

There was no one in the street. The air smelled strange. Meru had never been sick or known anyone who had, but some deep part of her knew what this was. Blood, vomit, and worse: bodies breaking down, voiding and bleeding and dying.

These were the sparks that the starwing had passed to Meru through the web, with an undertone of jangling wrongness. For every living thing it found, there were a hundred that had been living once. The walls around her, the houses that lined the street, were full of the dead.

The web refused to acknowledge them. When she searched with those parameters, it said, *Not found*, or else gave her yet another news report about a plague on a planet a hundred light-years away. There was no plague on Earth. The web said so.

But it was here. She could smell it. She *knew*.

Meru began to run.

Anyone sensible would have run away. Meru ran toward the place where Jian had been. Her thoughts were empty of anything but the need to be there, to see. To know. And then—

Then nothing. She could not think past it at all.

The place she ran to was near the heart of the sector. There, finally, were people: men and women sealed into space armor that sent off the signal of Consensus.

The starwing passed through the force field with no more than a shiver and a tingle as the energy fed its strange substance, and wrapped its wings around Meru. Inside that insubstantial shield, the starwing told her deep inside her mind, far below the oblivious hum of the web, she was invisible even to Consensus' sensors.

That was a disturbing thought, but the message that had brought Meru here was much worse. She slipped through the cordon of the Guard. The door to the tall grey house was open, and for a priceless few instants, no one guarded it.

It was dim inside. A lightstrip ran up the stair, shedding just enough pale green glow to guide Meru's feet. The landings along the way were deserted, the hallways dark. They smelled of the sickness, and of something heavier and sweeter.

That, she realized, was the smell of death. Her stomach heaved; she stumbled. There was a word in her head now, a simple word, the only word in this nightmare world: *No.*

The starwing's purr steadied her. She pulled herself upright. One more flight. One more landing. One last corridor, and a battered and broken door hanging half off its track.

The man who stood inside was not Jian, but Meru knew him as well as she knew her mother. He was her uncle, after all.

He saw her, which she had not expected. "Meru! What are you doing here?"

"Vekaa," she said, still stupid from the shock of what she had seen and smelled and sensed. "What—"

He moved to block the doorway. "Go now," he said. "Just go."

Meru would dearly have loved to do that. More than anything, she did not want to know what was in that room. But she had come all this way. Jian had called her. She had to know.

The starwing brushed Vekaa with the edge of a wing. He snapped back as if he had been struck with an energy bolt.

Meru wasted no time staring. She slipped past Vekaa, and stopped.

Jian was dead. Her face was empty. So was the web where she had been. The message was gone, the last synapse fired, the mind and consciousness dissolved.

The light was dim and Meru's sight kept blurring, but there was no mistaking the glistening red of blood that had trickled from ears and nostrils and eyes. Her hands were clenched into fists, her knees drawn up in a knot of pain.

Meru felt nothing at all. Not a single thing. There was so much to feel that there was no room in her for any of it.

Vekaa's body moved between them. This time the starwing let him be. Meru stared blankly up at him.

He looked like Jian. They all did in the family. He was Jian's brother; he had been the closest to her of any, except for Meru.

Meru could see no expression in his face. His eyes were sad, maybe. It was hard to tell. He was a scientist. He had been raised and trained to be coldly clinical.

She had been raised and trained to be a scientist, too. That was part of why she had gone so perfectly quiet inside.

She was observing, recording. Processing. Keeping a wall between herself and the tidal wave of feeling that would, eventually, drown her.

Her mother was dead. Something impossible, something no one could ever have planned for, had killed her.

"People don't get sick on this planet any more," Meru said. "They just don't. How did you let it happen?"

Vekaa made no effort to defend himself. "We don't know what it is," he said. "We do know that it's virulent, and powerfully contagious."

"She's not even supposed to be here," Meru said. Her walls were cracking. Her voice was trying to. "Why would she—"

"Please," Vekaa said. "I understand. When there's time, I'll listen, and mourn with you. But you have to leave this room. The Guard will take you to decontamination."

No, thought Meru. Oh, no. Absolutely not. She shook her head. "I'm already contaminated. I'm not leaving her."

"Every human being who has contracted this disease has died," Vekaa said. His voice was flat. "This sector has been sealed off with all who are in it, living or dead. Do you understand, Meru? You can't leave the sector until the seal is dissolved."

"Then I can stay here," Meru said.

"You can't," said Vekaa. Was his voice trying to crack, too? "You'll die."

The starwing hissed. Vekaa stiffened. So did Meru, who had never heard such a sound from it before.

The sound had meaning. Meru burst out with it before she stopped to think. "It says I won't die. It's protecting me."

Vekaa ignored her, or maybe he had not heard. Two large members of the Guard loomed on either side of her. They had weapons—here, Earthside, where weapons were banned.

She had not been thinking of all that this meant, only that her mother was here, and she was dead, and Meru could not—all the way down to the bone could not—leave her. Now understanding began to dawn, slow and brutal.

The web streamed knowledge of plagues on Earth and off, as far back as Meru could stand to go, overlaid with laws and defenses and restrictions that had kept Earth from enduring any such thing in over a thousand years. The laws were clear and uncompromising. Any plague that touched Earth, from any source offworld, was to be sealed off and eradicated without hesitation and without mercy, before it could spread beyond the spaceport where it began.

That was law. Reality was this tiny, dingy, antiquated room and the body abandoned in it. That dead thing had been Meru's mother, who should have been light-years away, safe and healthy and exploring an alien city.

The Guards moved in closer. Meru stilled the starwing before it tried something any of them might regret.

She was supposed to leave in two tendays—less than that, now: ride up the cable to the spaceport and then get on board a starship to the school for starpilots. She had devoted her life to getting there, and built all her hopes on it—and she had been accepted: one of only two on all of Earth this year, and one of a hundred from the known worlds.

It all seemed terribly remote now, and terribly unimportant. Meru had wanted the stars since she first began to remember—and much of that wanting was wrapped up in her mother.

Her mother was dead.

She reached out to the web and crashed headlong into a wall. She could see it, hear it, sense it through the implants that made her part of it. She could even detect the signal that was Yoshi, pinging and pinging again. But she was invisible and inaudible.

Then even that was gone. The silence was enormous. Meru was alone inside her own head.

While she talked to Vekaa, Consensus had finished locking down this whole sector and everyone in it. Meru cried out to her uncle with voice and data stream, but no answer came.

Every link, every connection, was cut off. The very root of it, the warm and constant presence that was the collective mind of her family, had vanished. Where it had been was nothing. Utter void. Absolute emptiness.

The shock was so great that it shut down her mind. She forgot how to resist. She could barely remember how to move.

The Guards herded her away from her mother's body, down the long flights of stairs and out into the bleak and empty street. She came to herself a little there, enough to eye paths of escape. But the starwing had gone dormant. Everywhere she turned was an armored Guard.

They meant this. There was no pleading they would hear, and no logic that would convince them. The only logic they knew was the order that sealed the plague away from the rest of Earth.

# Meredith

# Chapter 7

Holy crap.

I'd fallen asleep with my laptop in my lap. The clock by the side of my bed said *5:24*. For a long few seconds I couldn't remember what the numbers meant.

That wasn't a dream. That was memory. I had *lived* that night and day.

My throat was tight and my stomach wrenched with grief for someone else's mother. I'd been that someone else, living a life somewhere on the far side of time. I knew what death smelled like, and what a starwing was, and what it was like to feel the whole of the worlds-wide web inside my head.

How could I be remembering something that must be hundreds of years in the future? Memory only works one way. Everybody knows that.

*Alternate worlds.* Rick would say that, if I worked up the guts to tell him how far around the bend I was going. *Bubbles floating in a cosmic sea. Sometimes they touch. And when they do, for a few instants we can see. We can know…*

"Horse puckey," I said in my stuffy little room, where the air conditioning never really worked right, and the ceiling fan could whip up a gale. "I'm suffering from writer's psychosis. That's what it is. Stories gone bad. Taking over my head. Mom will say I'd do anything to get out of going to Egypt."

And then she'd make me go anyway. Mom doesn't give up once she makes her mind up to something. I could be straight-out barking crazy and she'd just shovel me through security in my nice white coat with the nice tight straps.

I didn't feel crazy. I felt gutted, because I'd just seen my mother dead and lost everything I—the other I—knew. But my mind was clear. Everything around me, now I was wide awake, made sense. Or as much sense as anything ever does.

I skated along over the top of the dream or memory or whatever it was. I got dressed up, went out, ate rock shrimp and fried grouper and hush puppies, and Mom didn't ask me if anything was wrong. I wasn't *that* good an actor. Was I?

By the time we got home I was almost back to abnormal. Cat and Rick were waiting on the patio with flashlights, armed and ready for turtle watch. Rick was texting with Greg as usual. Cat was stargazing, also as usual.

Sometimes Mom came, too. Tonight she said, "I'm too full to move. You go, do us proud. Happy counting!"

I swapped out dinner clothes for shorts and a tank and my beach shoes, caught a drive-by Mom kiss and headed for the beach.

We do turtle watch for the community college every summer. In May and June we go down to the beach after dark, when the sea turtles come up out of the surf. They dig their nests and lay their eggs, and we count them for the community college. Then in July and August when the eggs hatch, we go back again and count the ones that survive, and watch as the tiny turtles make their bound and determined way toward the ocean.

I had the map of the beach up on my phone—already marked in a dozen places where we'd seen turtles making nests in the past week or so—and the app was ready to start counting as soon as a turtle came in. It was early for turtles: the sky was dark, but the horizon over the mainland was stained blood-red with the last of the sunset.

The air wrapped around me like a warm blanket. For a few seconds it felt impossibly strange, as if I'd been expecting the biting cold I'd felt in my dream. Memory. Whatever.

The sound of the ocean was the same in the dream and out of it. The long slow heave and sigh was louder than usual tonight. "Must be a storm out to sea," Cat said.

Rick grunted. It was a comfortable sound. Familiar. Friendly.

The waves were high, and the moon was up, shining down a long silver road like the road from Meru's island to the spaceport. The foam glowed white against the black water. It was so beautiful it hurt.

I was homesick already, and I hadn't even left for Egypt yet. Cat and Rick headed off down the beach in opposite directions—covering as much territory as possible. That left me to hold the middle.

I sat on the steps down below the dunes, next to a sea grape that rustled and creaked in the wind off the ocean. When I looked down at my hands in the moonlight, they looked like someone else's. I was half expecting them to be long and thin and the color of black coffee, like Meru's. These shorter, fatter, whitey-brown things didn't make sense to me at all.

Bonnie, Mom, Egypt, the dream that was so real, were all tangled up in my head. I couldn't tell anybody about it, even Cat, who knew everything else about me. What could I say? Nothing made any sense.

While my mind spun its wheels, my eyes scanned the surf. Dark things floated in the foam—a log, an escaped buoy, a clump of seaweed trapped in plastic.

One thing wasn't like the others. It was solid and rounded, and it moved against the thrust of the wave. It washed up on the beach just past the foot of the steps, rocking when the wave tried to suck it back.

The turtle didn't pause to get its bearings, the way most of them did. It was already moving, fighting against the weight of the air, digging flippers in and dragging itself forward.

It was a big one, as big as I was, but much heavier. It left a deep trail cross-hatched with flipper tracks, right up past the foot of the steps.

I saw the water dripping from its shell, and the knots of weeds and barnacles, and the pale line of a scar from the middle to the edge. This turtle had come a long, hard way to lay its eggs.

Out of the water it was almost blind. As long as I didn't move, it couldn't see me. With what for a sea turtle was serious speed, it dug in its hind flippers and sent sand flying, digging the hole for its nest.

It was right beside me. I could see its face, and its big scarred head. The moon glimmered on the tears that ran down its cheeks, ran and ran, all the while it made its nest and laid its round white eggs. My finger on the phone's screen counted each plop as a new egg landed on top of the rest.

It didn't even know I was there, or if it knew, it didn't care. I counted ninety-six plops before the turtle paddled sand over them all, burying them as deep as it could. Then it kicked and struggled itself around to face the water.

It went back fast. They always do that: slow coming in, as if the weight of eggs and earth is too much for them, but quick going back, as if they can't wait to be home again.

It hesitated just before the wave rolled in. Bracing itself, like Meru before she stepped onto the road. Then the water caught it and lifted it up, suddenly weightless, and carried it away.

# Meritre

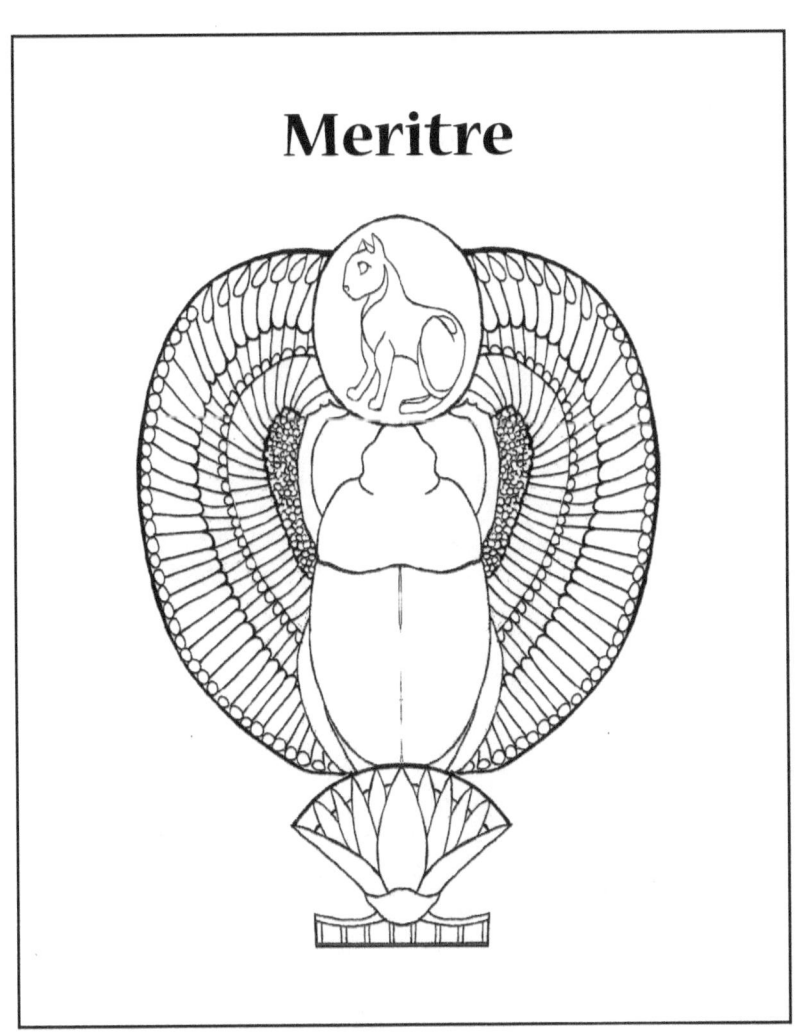

# Chapter 8

Meritre had had visions since she was small. Sometimes she could see what would happen, or hear or feel it. Sometimes she lived another life, a life full of metal birds that flew across the sky, and nights full of stars that looked almost familiar, but not quite. And sometimes when the night was quiet or the sun was so blinding bright at midday that everyone took shelter to escape from it, she heard the gods speaking to one another.

She almost never spoke of it. She had no desire to become a soothsayer in the market, and since she was neither a king nor a high-ranking priest, there was not much use in it except occasionally to awe her brothers.

She had seen the plague in nightmares, night after night, but she had also seen that it would end. She had clung to that through the worst of it. The world would go on. The people would survive. There would still be a king in the palace and crocodiles in the river, and the sun would beat down at noon and give way at night to the patterns of stars that she had known all her life.

Since the plague retreated, the visions had finally let her be. If she could have wished for one, it would be of her mother and father safe and healthy, and the new baby safely born and blessed with a long and prosperous life. But her gift from the gods had never been that easily controlled.

Meritre was in no mood to lie back and let the gods tell her what they intended to do. She was not in a mood for prayer, either. Prayer might have kept the family safe through the plague, but with Father ill and Mother expecting a baby at her age and in her fragile condition, Meritre dared leave nothing to chance.

She needed magic.

The world was full of it. Even before gods, magic had been; all creation had been born of it. From the charm a woman laid on a man to make him love her to the spell a physician worked to heal an illness, magic made certain what prayer could only hope for.

It did not always work. If Meritre was honest with herself, it often failed.

She had to try. Thanks to Uncle Amonmose who was a scribe in the palace, she had learned to read and even write a little. Also thanks to him, she had a book of her own, made up of scraps that he had given her to practice writing on. Some of the scraps had bits of spells and charms written on them already, and she had made a point of adding to them when she could.

They were mostly minor: how to conjure away a wart, charm a fish onto a hook, or call a breeze on a hot day. But some could be more than that.

She was not arrogant enough to try the great magic, to raise the dead or force the gods to serve her. She only wanted to protect her family. For that, there were more than enough spells; the difficulty was to choose the right one.

The king's festival was still a handful of days away, but the gods had been looking out for Meritre. That day Aweret had been able to go to the temple and join the choir for its practice, and while she had been somewhat pale and shaky, her beautiful voice had made them all whole again. Then in the evening Uncle Amonmose came by for dinner, bringing with him one of the young scribes it was his duty to train.

Djehuti was tall and quiet, with long, sensitive hands that curled around a cup with unconscious grace. He never said much, but Meritre could tell his eyes and ears took in everything around him. He was a quick learner, Uncle Amonmose said; he had mastered all the books of the younger scribes' course, and was almost ready to take on his own students.

Meritre had met him a time or two before. She liked the way he had of being so very much there, but not chattering about it. After her brothers, who never stopped talking even when they were asleep, it was wonderfully restful.

That evening after everyone had eaten, they all sat on the roof, watching the last blood-red light fade from the western sky. There was a brisk breeze off the river; it had blown away the biting flies. People were on their roofs all over the city, talking back and forth, laughing and singing. It was a little festival of its own, a celebration that they were alive.

Meritre left the men to their noise and chatter and want to sit by the roof's edge, as close to the western horizon as she could go. After a moment or two and a little to her surprise, Djehuti came over and sat beside her.

He did not try to talk to her. He simply sat there with the wind in his face. His smooth skull, shaved for cleanliness as every scribe's was, had a pleasing shape to it in the last of the light. His face was pleasing, too, without being so pretty it made her blush: long clean lines, dark level brows, firm but rounded chin.

Any other time, she might have enjoyed looking at it until there was no more light to see with. Tonight she had too much on her mind.

Something about his silence drew words out of her. "I need advice," she said, "about magic. I need a spell to protect everybody here. There are so many, and I'm not sure—"

"Why?"

The word hung in the warm darkness. Behind them, Father and Uncle Amonmose and the boys were well into the beer.

The cat appeared out of the night and established itself in Meritre's lap. Its purring and the softness of its fur under her fingers helped her answer his question. "I want to keep my family safe."

There was enough lamplight from the other side of the roof to see his shape but little else. She heard him breathing. After a while he said, "Something's troubling you."

"It's not a new plague," Meritre said quickly. "I just want to do this."

"You didn't do it during the plague?"

"I didn't have to. The gods did it instead. Now they have other things to do, and I've been studying. I can't guard the whole kingdom. I'm not that powerful, and I wouldn't presume. But this household I can protect."

He paused for a very long time, until she was sure he was not going to respond, even to refuse. Then he said, "There are incantations that are as safe as magic ever is, that don't require months to prepare, or ingredients that only a king can afford. Do you need them quickly?"

"As soon as can be," Meritre said.

He hugged his knees and rocked. "Tomorrow evening I think I can get away."

Meritre's heart swelled to fill her chest, making it hard to breathe. But her mind was clear enough for her to say, "Don't come here. People will ask questions. Meet me in the market by the amulet seller's stall."

There were several of those in the market nearest the house, Meritre remembered too late, but Djehuti brushed with his finger the blue scarab she wore around her neck. "I know the one," he said. "I'll be there."

Now that Meritre had made up her mind to do something, she felt strangely relieved. There was fear, of course, and a quiver of excitement, but most of all, it felt right. She slept well that night, barely interrupted by Father's coughing and the yowl of mating cats in the street outside.

The dream ambushed her just before dawn. She was aware that it was a dream, and that it was true. At first she thought it was a memory of the past: the plague was at its height, death and dying in every house, and those who cared for the dead were dying themselves, of exhaustion as much as of the plague.

That was as she remembered, but she had lived in the midst of it then. Now she stood high above it under a sky full of stars. Death stalked the city below her and the fields that surrounded it, and filled the river with the helpless dead, until the crocodiles could eat no more.

She lifted her hand. The stars dimmed; the earth held its breath. The flood of death began to ebb, slowly at first, then more quickly.

When she lowered her hand, the plague had gone in all but one place. Down below her in the sleeping city, death claimed one final sacrifice. That life, the last one, lay like the petal of a flower in Meritre's palm.

As she stared down at it, it shriveled and shrank, closing upon itself. When it was no more than a smudge of dust, a breath of wind caught and lifted it and carried it away, spiraling upward until it vanished among the stars.

# Meredith

# Chapter 9

All the way from Orlando to New York to Egypt on the long, long flights, I kept sliding in and out of that other life, the one with the cat and the temple and the family in its mud-brick house in the middle of a hundred other mud-brick houses, and that other me standing as tall as the sky. There was a hawk above me, wings spread wide, soaring through the blue heaven.

Except to me, it didn't look like a hawk. It looked like the jet I was riding in, with its hawk-of-Horus logo on the tail. It was red and gold and blue, and it looked like ancient Egypt.

I was a little excited by then. A little. All right?

Cat would mock me, but there wasn't any wi-fi on this flight. I was flying blind, with a tablet full of books and music and the craziness inside my own head. I'd have to wait till I landed before I could hook myself back up to the world.

I'd stopped fighting by the time Mom gave me one last rib-creaking hug outside of the airport security gate. "Just six weeks," she said. "Then everything can get back to normal."

Whatever normal was. I hefted the backpack full of laptop and supplies for the trip and the shiny new tablet that everybody had got together with Mom to give me for a going-away present, and said before Mom could say it again, for the sixteen dozenth time, "Yes, I've got my passport and my visa and my boarding passes and my global phone card and—"

"And your head screwed on firmly and all relevant numbers saved to every electronic device and the notebook in your pocket," Mom finished for me. "Be safe. Behave. Don't forget to Skype."

I could still smell her perfume through the stale and slightly cold smell of airplane air. It wrapped around me like her hug. When I dozed off I could feel her beside me.

*That* was a dream. Reality was a long, long flight from morning into night and then into morning again.

On the last leg of the trip, from Cairo to Luxor, I looked down and saw what Meritre's hawk must have been seeing. I didn't see the place I'd been dreaming or remembering, at least not the way it was in the dream. The city I was about to land in was the same kind of smoky sprawl you see everywhere else you go—except for all the ruins poking out of it.

The river was there. So was the way the green parts stayed close to the water, and the rest of the world was bare red-brown desert. That hadn't changed much in however many thousand years.

I was wide awake, so tired I couldn't remember what sleep felt like. I missed Mom and Bonnie and the usuals deep inside, like a bruise that wouldn't heal. Mom had e-mailed me once, and we'd texted back and forth every time I was on the ground.

Then in New York I got an actual pleasant surprise: the whole barn had a Skype party for me. They linked up Rick's tablet and hauled it around the barn and showed me all the horses, and Bonnie got it all smeary when she drooled hay foam on it.

I promised them all to write down everything and take pictures everywhere—starting with a picture of the terminal I was in. I wished I could send them the dreams, too. They were so real I could still feel the cat's fur under my hand, and taste the stew Meritre had made in that last dream, the one with the boy she liked so much it made her toes curl.

The stew was good. So was the bread when it came out of the oven, though it was grainier than the grainiest whole-grain bread I'd ever gnawed my way through. No butter, either. But it was tasty dipped in the stew.

My mouth was watering. Soda and peanuts didn't quite come up to it, but they filled my stomach, which was more than dream food could do.

I hadn't dreamed or remembered Meru again. I admit I was glad. Meritre's life wasn't easy, but the grief in it was either worn down with age or it hadn't happened yet. Meru's grief was right there, lodged like a knife in my gut.

The flight attendant who'd been keeping an eye on me came by and made sure my seat back was up and my tray was stowed for landing and all those other things I already knew. I didn't tell her that. She was too honestly nice, and I loved her accent. It was worth it just to listen to the way her tongue curled around the English words.

I wished she'd slide into Arabic so I could hear what she really sounded like, but she never did. I had to listen to the PA for that. All the announcements were in Arabic as well as English.

When the plane was down and we were all herded through Customs and I was the only dirty-blonde-haired person anywhere in sight, it hit me right between the sort-of-blue-sort-of-grey-sort-of-green eyes. This place was *foreign*. And what the hell was I doing in it?

I started to freak out. What if Aunt Jessie had the wrong time for my flight? What if she couldn't make it to pick me up and hadn't been able to call? What if—

"Meredith!"

I'd know that voice anywhere. Aunt Jessie had a hat jammed down over her rusty-colored curls, and her clothes were straight out of Indiana Jones: boots and khakis and a loose white shirt. No tank tops out in public in this country—she'd made sure I knew that before I left.

Her hug swallowed me up. I hugged back so hard she went *Oof.* I still hadn't forgiven her, not hardly, but right then the only person I'd have been gladder to see was Mom.

She rounded up my luggage and introduced me to the two people with her—both grad students and both from Egypt, with the same accent the flight attendant had—and herded us all out to an honest-to-Horus Land Rover. I used to dream about riding through the desert in a Land Rover.

Not that Luxor's desert, exactly. It's Black Land: riverside Egypt, about as humid as Florida, and about as buggy, too. But there's desert around it, and across the river where the tombs are.

Ancient Egypt is everywhere. Statues, temples, rows of columns cropping up next to a street that could have come right out of Palm Bay: no matter where you turn, there's something to remind you that three, four, five thousand years ago, people were here. Right here, where you're sitting in a traffic jam in your aunt's Land Rover, with tourists clogging every street and bazaar, and vendors selling everything from genuine reproduction antique amulets to cans of Coca-Cola.

I bought an amulet while we sat waiting for the street to clear, off a tray of them. It was just like the one Meritre wore in my dream, a blue beetle on a string. "Stops Evil Eye," the man who sold it said. I got him to repeat that in Arabic, so I could start learning what people were really saying.

"That's a scarab," Aunt Jessie said, "but you know that, don't you? Do you know what it says on the bottom? *May Isis grant healing.*"

In my dream it helped people fend off the plague. I wondered if it could fend off cancer, too.

Meritre believed in magic. I just wrote stories about it. I hung the scarab around my neck under my shirt.

Aunt Jessie's expedition worked out of Luxor House, right by the river and the ferry across to the desert and the tombs. On the outside it was a blank white wall with a gate painted brilliant turquoise. Inside was a chain of courtyards and a whole lot of rooms and labs and classrooms and a dining hall, and a library that took up a whole wing.

I called dibs on the library, but first I had to move into my room. Because the digging season was over for everybody but us, I had it to myself. I put up the actual hardcopy picture of me and Mom and the one of me on Bonnie and the one with all the usuals from the midwinter show at the barn, tacked up the map of the Valley of the Kings that I'd got out of one of Dad's *National Geographic*s from before I was born, plugged all my tech in to charge and made sure the house wi-fi would talk to it, and that was as close to home as I was going to get.

While I was unpacking my wheelie duffel, Cat shot me a text. *Now tell me you hate it.*

I shot straight back. *Love Luxor. Hate how I got here.*

*That's fair,* she said. Then she sent me a picture of Bonnie and Dora giving each other scritchies in the pasture. Bonnie had to stretch her neck to reach Dora's withers, because Dora is a good foot taller than she is, but she still managed to look almost as big on the outside as she is on the inside.

*Stop making me homesick,* I said.

*Don't be,* Cat answered. *Dig up a mummy for me.*

*Keep bugging me and I'll ship you a cat mummy just to shut you up,* I said.

*Oooo!* she said. *Do it! I dare you!*

*Maybe not a cat. Baboon.*

*Triple cat dare!*

*Not in three lifetimes,* I said.

I don't know why I shivered. Must have been a draft.

Aunt Jessie had told me to go to bed and sleep off the jet lag, but I couldn't sit still. I took a shower and changed my clothes, and that was almost as good as sleep. Then I wandered out.

A cat attached itself to me outside the door. It was a little round tortoiseshell cat with a marking like a flame on her forehead, and extra toes, so she looked as if she had thumbs. She didn't look anything like Meritre's sleek brown cat, but she had the same eyes, ancient and self-satisfied and wise.

I could never have a cat at home: Mom was deathly allergic. Having one find me here made up for a lot of things, though not nearly all of them.

I scratched her chin and she mewped at me. When I went on she went, too, following from in front the way cats do.

I meant to go down and find the door to the library, but with the cat for company, I found myself going up instead. The house had two floors and a roof, and the roof was a garden.

There were orange and lemon trees up there, more pots of flowers that I could count, and a kind of gazebo with a couch in it and a clutter of chairs.

The roof had a wall around it, low enough for me to lean on. With the sun shining straight into my eyes, I couldn't see much of the river or the cliffs on the other side, so I turned and looked across the city instead.

There was an excavation right below the house, in between it and a neighborhood of shops and hotels and what looked like apartment buildings. I don't know why I hadn't expected that. They were still digging right in the middle of the main temple, the temple of Amon, Aunt Jessie had told me on the way from the airport, and finding new things in places that had been dug and re-dug for two hundred years.

This wasn't anything so spectacular: just rows of trenches and the straight lines of walls with breaks that might be doors. I knew enough to think it must have been a neighborhood like the modern one on the other side of it. If I squinted just right, I could see how the houses went down in rows, with a street in the middle, and an alley that ran right up to the wall of the house I was in.

Suddenly I was so dizzy I had to grab the wall to keep from falling down. I don't know what did it—the angle of the light, the way one wall met another, or maybe it was that I looked up at just the right instant and saw the exact line of hills across the river that Meritre saw when she stood on the roof of her house.

If I closed my eyes I could see the rows of mud-brick houses, some of which had gardens on the roofs, and most had tents or shades for people to sleep under when the weather was hot. There was no huge temple of Amon yet: the one Meritre sang in was bright and new, but it wasn't any bigger than the mosque I could see from Luxor House.

I could see it, feel it, hear it, *smell* it: smoke and sweat and sicky-sweet perfume, baking bread and sour beer and a really tasty lentil stew with onions in it.

That was ancient Thebes, capital of Upper Egypt, but Luxor was there, too, with motor exhaust and cooking oil and flowers. It was Luxor I opened my eyes to. Thebes was gone except for the bare outline of streets and houses.

I clutched the scarab amulet so tight it dug into my palm. I must have seen a photo of the excavation somehow, with one of those artist's recreations drawn over it. The other things, the smells and sounds, were too much imagination and my stomach telling me it was ready for dinner.

I hoped that was what it was. Because what else could it be? Reincarnation?

*Hello, this is your past life speaking. Sorry you weren't Cleopatra, but some kind of singing priestess isn't bad.*

Singer of Amon. That's what I'd seen, been, whatever. The way I knew that was like the way Meru rode the web, which was her world's version of the Internet, more or less, but instead of a computer she had a chip in her brain that connected her to it. All I had to do was think a question, and the answer was there.

The cat wrapped herself around my ankles once, twice, and then a third time to make sure the job got done. Then she jumped onto the wall and butted her head against my arm. She was purring so hard her whole body shook.

She didn't start talking. That was a good thing. I rubbed the soft fur behind her ears while she went nuts, purring and leaning into my fingers.

I liked it that she was just being a cat. I needed her to be normal and ordinary and everyday.

The sun sank so low it touched the horizon, and the mosquitoes started to come out. They might not be sparrow-sized like Florida mosquitoes, but there were ten zillion of them. They drove me off the roof.

# Meredith

# Chapter 10

After all that, I slept like the dead. If there were dreams, or whatever else my crazy brain was doing to me, I didn't remember them. The alarm knocked me out of bed and into the dig clothes Aunt Jessie had ordered me to get, and while I wasn't the first one down to breakfast in the dark before dawn, I wasn't the last one, either.

I grew up listening to Aunt Jessie's stories and looking at pictures of hot, dusty, grinning people holding up bits of pottery or chips of old bones. King Tut's gold is a once-in-a-century kind of find. Mostly, archaeology is dirt and potsherds. And digging. They call it a dig for good reason.

Now, like it or not, I was inside one of Aunt Jessie's stories. She'd really meant it about putting me to work. She was going to the site this morning, and that meant so was I. Jet lag or no jet lag.

There were six of us at breakfast: Aunt Jessie and me and three grad students, the two I'd met yesterday plus two Americans who were so obviously a couple they might as well have been wearing matching collars. They were wearing pretty much the same pants and shirts and hats, but so were the rest of us. It was a uniform.

At that hour nobody had much to say except the occasional grunt around a cup of coffee. I got names—Gwyn and Jonathan, those were the Americans—and Gwyn sort of smiled in my general direction, but mostly we were all half-asleep.

When we were all fed and caffeinated, we trudged out to the two Land Rovers we'd be riding in, both of them loaded with gear. There was just about enough room for the six of us to squeeze in around it.

Nobody was particularly nice to me, but they weren't hazing me, either. They were treating me like everybody else. That was a compliment. I think. Or else they were just too sleepy to care.

I ended up wedged in between Gwyn and a large and lumpy duffel. It was still dark out, but somewhere a bird had woken up and started to holler. We set off down the street in the predawn cool.

In Florida after the sun goes down the heat just gets lighter and the sun stops pressing on your head. In Egypt, once you get away from the river, it's almost cold in the early morning, enough to need long sleeves to keep the warmth in. Then once the sun comes up, you need them to keep the heat out.

We crossed the river in the very first glimmer of light, and from various points on both sides of the water, we heard a rhythmic wailing sound with words winding through it. Amira and the other Egyptian student, Hamid, got out of the Land Rovers and spread little rugs on the deck of the ferry and started kneeling and bowing, both in the same direction, like just about everyone else on the boat. It was time for prayer in this part of the world, and I'd heard the muezzin calling the faithful to do their duty.

I didn't remember it from last night, though I had to have heard it. I must have slept through it.

My cell phone whinnied. I jumped. So did Gwyn—then she laughed.

Damn. I had to change that ringtone.

I unlocked the phone. There was a whole stack of messages, hours old, besides the newest one: a text from Mom. *Up yet? Digging yet?*

The breath rushed out of me. I hadn't even known I was holding it. *Crossing the Nile,* I texted back.

*Call me later,* she said. *Will be up for a while.*

She was headed toward the end of yesterday. I was just at the beginning of today. That's the magic of time zones.

It felt like my dreams, a bit. I had a brief, overpowering urge to call her and tell her what was happening to me. She might not get it, either, but she'd listen. Mom always listened. Even if she ended up doing the exact opposite of what I wanted her to.

I couldn't bring myself to do it. *Later,* I texted, and put the phone away.

Sunrise found us on the road away from the Nile. No matter what I thought about how I'd got here, I couldn't hold on to that now. Maybe this was Mom's dream, and damn her for not taking it for herself, but I'd grown up with it, too.

This was it. I was here. These bare hills, these steep ridges and sandy valleys, were *the* place to be an archaeologist.

There weren't any Pyramids here—those were all the way up near Cairo—but there were temples and tombs and hieroglyphs everywhere you'd want to look.

"Almost there," Gwyn said as if she could read my mind. "We're working in the Valley of the Queens—in the ruins of a temple that your aunt helped discover when she was in grad school. Over the past twenty years her expeditions have dug most of it out, and started on the maze of tunnels beneath. We don't know yet how far those go."

"Far," said Aunt Jessie from the driver's seat. "Tomb robbers used them, of course, to get into the tombs nearby. But they're the same age as the temple. We're still not sure exactly what they were meant for."

"A tomb, of course," Gwyn said. "What else could it be?"

"We can't be sure," said Aunt Jessie. "Not without better evidence than we've found. And even if it was a tomb, it most likely was robbed long ago. Or priests emptied it before the robbers could, to protect and preserve the royal mummies, if not the goods they were buried with."

That argument was worn smooth around the edges. Even I could tell that, from the way Gwyn rolled her eyes. "Yes, Professor. Of course, Professor."

"Watch your heads," Aunt Jessie said.

I don't know if she was trying to ding Gwyn for being rude, but she hauled the Land Rover around a corner, nearly bouncing us both out through the roof, and there it was. If I'd had any breath left to catch, I would have caught it.

A cliff reared up ahead of us, cutting off the glare of the rising sun. The temple sat at its base. It wasn't nearly as ruined as I'd expected; it had a definite shape, with the stumps of columns marching down two sides, though the roof was gone.

I reached for my phone to snap a picture, but nobody was getting it this morning: there was no signal. That gave me the horrors for a minute. Or two or maybe six.

I wouldn't be getting any sympathy here. I put my phone away, and took a deep breath. I could do this. I could even make myself like it. I just had to think about Cat, and how she would give just about anything to be here.

I wished she was. But that wasn't doing anybody any good, either.

The excavation crew was already at it when we got there: men and boys whose families had been digging in this valley since archaeology was invented.

"Most of them were tomb robbers before that," Gwyn said. She was my supervisor, and her job was to teach me how to label potsherds and log them into the expedition's database.

That meant we got to sit in a tent, out of the heat and the worst of the dust, and she had a tablet but I had to write everything down on paper. Backup, you know. Aunt Jessie was old school.

I hoped I'd graduate to actual digging, but that was skilled work, and I wasn't ready for it yet. As the morning went on and the heat rose up and up, I didn't mind being able to do my job in the shade.

It wasn't as boring as you might think. Potsherds are broken pieces of pots. When you're digging in ancient places, they're everywhere, and they're really important if you're an archaeologist. You can tell all kinds of things about a place and a time and a people by the dishes and jars and cups they left behind.

These had bits of bright color on them, and some had hieroglyphs or fragments of pictures: a bird's head, a peacock's feather, a woman's hand. I loved handling them, and I didn't mind pasting tiny little number codes on the backs. Back in the lab at Luxor House, the pot people would take each piece and put it together like a puzzle, and eventually they'd end up with all or most of a pot.

Once or twice, for a sort of treat, I got to label a glass bead, and once an amulet so much like the one I was wearing that I dropped it in surprise. Lucky for me, it only fell three inches to the table. Gwyn didn't even look up.

I don't know why my hand was shaking so much. Scarabs are as common as sand in Egypt. The one I was logging had the same inscription as mine, but so did half the scarabs in the country.

It was just me being all jet-lagged and weird. I couldn't keep the scarab, of course, and I didn't ask. I labeled and logged it and put it in the box with a dozen others like it.

Well, not exactly like it. The others were nice enough, and some were nicer. That particular one just felt right when I touched it. So right it freaked me out.

"What happens to all these things?" I asked Gwyn. "Do they end up in a museum?"

She looked up from the tablet, stretched and sighed. "Too much of what everyone finds gets studied and noted, then the Department of Antiquities takes it away. Mostly it disappears into boxes in the museum in Cairo. If it's a tomb with a mummy in it, the mummy goes back in the tomb with a few of the grave goods. Sometimes, if an expedition is really lucky, the site gets its own museum. That's what we're hoping for here. We've been getting grants, and your aunt has brought in some rich donors. We almost have enough to get started."

"That's kind of a big deal, isn't it?"

"Kind of," she said.

I don't think she was laughing at me. I bent back down to my potsherds.

The heat mounted; even in the shade, it got so we could barely breathe. Gwyn had to shut the tablet down before it fried its innards.

That was like a signal. The work outside stopped. We gathered our bits and pieces together and locked them in boxes and helped load them in the Land Rovers. Whatever was left to do would wait until tomorrow, with guards to make sure it didn't get stolen before then.

The light outside, just at noon, was blinding even through Florida-strength sunglasses. I'd thought it was hot in the tent. It was a blast furnace in the sun.

When I took a breath, the inside of my nose burned. My eyes felt all crackly. My clothes were hotter than I was.

"A hundred and twelve degrees," Aunt Jessie said as she started up the Land Rover. "We're having a cold snap. It was a hundred and twenty-six last week."

All I could manage was a kind of strangled moan. The Land Rover had air conditioning, thank God, or should I say thank Horus? What they say about dry heat in the desert—they aren't kidding. I wasn't even sweating. Any sweat I could squeeze out evaporated before I could feel it.

Jonathan handed me a bottle of lukewarm water. Gwyn had been making me drink every fifteen minutes by the clock, and I'd been taking pee breaks at just about that speed, but I was parched.

The water tasted like plastic, but underneath it I could swear I tasted the thin and sour but weirdly solid taste of ancient Egyptian beer.

# Meredith

# Chapter 11

The Land Rover bumped and grumbled down the road to the ferry. I still had the water bottle in my hand, half full, and people were talking around me about heat and lunch and digging in the sand. Inside of me was this whole other world.

Luxor House was cool and dim and made me want to tumble straight into sleep, but I was starved. We ate lunch in the corner of the dining hall closest to the kitchen, gulping down gallons of iced tea and diving into platters of sandwiches and big bowls of salad and pitas and hummus.

The rest of the hall had a weird little echo, as if all the people who would have been in it during the regular season were still there. It wasn't anything like the echo in my head.

Aunt Jessie and Amira and the others were talking about the tunnels they were excavating under the temple, going back and forth on how big it all really was, how old it was, and who had built it. Apparently today they'd found an inscription that had Jonathan and Hamid in a lather, but Aunt Jessie, as usual, wasn't quite ready to commit.

"You know it is!" Jonathan insisted. He was a stocky guy, but quick and surprisingly light on his feet, and when he got excited he bounced. The first time I saw him do it, I had to fight not to laugh.

He was bouncing now, stabbing the last of the hummus with a wedge of pita and glaring at Aunt Jessie. "It's right there in the cartouche. It *is* Tawosret."

"Maybe," Aunt Jessie said. She can drive you crazy being noncommittal, and she was doing a good job of it now. "It's fragmentary, and there are other interpretations. If this was a woman pharaoh, she'd have made sure to build her tomb and temple in the Valley of the Kings, not here with the queens."

"So she built it for someone else," Gwyn said. "Mother, maybe."

"Daughter," I said.

That came straight out of nowhere. I froze, hoping they were too busy arguing to notice, but of course they heard.

They all turned to stare at me. I braced to be jumped on, but even Aunt Jessie nodded. "That's possible," she said. "We know she had a son who died before he could father an heir, which left her to rule as king. She very likely had a daughter as well."

I bit my tongue. Of course she had a daughter—one she loved with her whole heart and soul, and raised to be king. I knew that the way I knew what Egyptian beer tasted like.

"There's no historical record of such a person," Amira said, "and mortuary temples weren't built for wives or children. They were built for the king. This must have another purpose."

"Such as?" Gwyn demanded.

Amira shrugged. "Who knows? Maybe she wanted to honor the queens who went before her."

"Guilt?" Gwyn said. "Because she got to be king and they didn't?"

"More likely she'd want to let them know she'd attained godhood," said Amira.

"Thumbing her nose at them for all eternity?" Gwyn looked downright offended.

Aunt Jessie's voice came in between them before the argument got any uglier. "That's enough, you two. There's an answer somewhere in there, I'm sure. The more we excavate, the more we'll find. Maybe we'll finally find the tomb."

As a distraction, that worked beautifully. They all sighed, even Aunt Jessie.

When archaeologists dream, they dream of being the first person to open a new and—that's the next to impossible part—unrobbed tomb. Everybody's heard about King Tut, because he's the only pharaoh who survived all those thousands of years without being found and cleaned out.

That doesn't stop anybody from hoping there's another one out there somewhere. Even an empty tomb, or better yet, one that still has its mummy in it, is enough to get an Egyptologist excited.

Everybody wandered off after that. They had work to do in the lab or the library, and I had orders to take a nap.

I was more than ready to fall over. I left two messages first. One for Mom, just a ping and a *Love you.* And one for Cat and Rick and Kristen: *Still alive. Miss you.* The rest could wait till I woke up.

Once I was horizontal under the mosquito netting, with the ceiling fan blowing cool air over me and the little tortie cat purring on the pillow beside my ear, my brain came wide awake. The more I tried to fall asleep, the less sleepy I was.

I reached for my phone. Changed my mind. Pulled the laptop over instead.

I started an email to the usuals. *Trip Report,* I typed. *Rock the First.*

It was all in my head, starting with the flights and the airport and Aunt Jessie and the grad students and everything else that had happened since. What came out was completely different.

*I think I'm going crazy. But it feels real. Like there are three of me, living at three different ends of time.*

I could imagine what Rick would say to that. Something about physics. And psychiatry. Kristen would talk right past me about boys and horse shows. Cat would tell me that was a nice start for a story, but what about Egypt?

I typed an answer to her, sort of. *I keep thinking about the temple and the woman king. She wanted her daughter to be king, too. But she built a temple for her where the queens were buried. Aunt Jessie thinks that means the princess died before her mother.*

*The thing is—I know she did.*

*All these people have been dead for thousands of years. But I can feel the sadness as if it happened yesterday. I feel Meritre in the middle of her vision, seeing that one last life the plague will take before it stops, and realizing no magic she can make will change what she sees. She doesn't know yet which life that is, but I do. I know.*

*I know it the way I know what I had for breakfast yesterday, and what Bonnie's mane smells like, and how to get from bio lab to Language Arts at school.*

*That's got to be jet lag, right? How old do you have to be before schizophrenia starts?*

"Maybe it's a brain tumor," Kristen said helpfully in my head. Besides boys and dressage shows, Kristen's other obsession is medicine.

*Right,* I said with my fingers. *It will be Mom's turn to go crazy worrying about me, and my turn to do the chemo and the wig and the nightmares.*

I shut off that thought before it went any further. I didn't feel sick. I didn't feel crazy, either, though that didn't necessarily mean anything.

*Suppose I'm not imagining things. Suppose I really am living someone else's life. Time travel, magic—who knows what it is? I don't have to believe in magic for it to be real, do I?*

Meritre believed. She was still working on a spell to save her family from another round of the plague. Maybe it wouldn't work. But maybe it would.

*What if—*

I shut that thought off, too. If magic could cure cancer, someone would have done it a long, long time ago.

*Still,* I typed, *what if it could work? What if that's what I'm doing here? Time traveling in my head, with this weird connection an ancient Egyptian person who happens to be just about the same age I am?*

My fingers went still on the keys. What if I could find a spell that would make sure Mom never came out of remission ever?

As long as I was thinking impossible things, I couldn't help but make the leap to the other side of time.

*What if Meru is real, too? She's thousands of years in the future. Science is so far advanced it might as well be magic. They* must *have cured cancer. Didn't she say no one gets sick any more? Got. Will get. Damn, this is complicated.*

Rick in my head, always the practical one, pointed out what I already knew. "Even if it is real, and you really are the midpoint of two lives at the far ends of time, what good will it do? All you can do is watch. You can't communicate with them."

*Can't I?*

The scarab swung on its string around my neck. I closed my hand over it to make it stop.

*Meritre has one like it. The one I logged in the tent can't be that one, can it?*

*What if it is?*

"Crazy," I said.

"So?" Now my head gave me Cat, playing along. "If it is Meritre's amulet, maybe it can help you communicate somehow. After all, what good is time travel if you can't talk to each other? Are you supposed to just watch your separate train wrecks and not be able to do a thing about it?"

I stared at the disjointed mess on the laptop screen. Anybody I sent that to would be calling Aunt Jessie and telling her to get me some help—stat, as Kristen would say.

I hit Delete.

*Are you really sure you want to delete this message?* the computer asked.

There was one way to find out if I was right. I knew more or less where artifact storage was. If I was lucky, the box of scarabs would still be out in the open; someone had to double-check its contents against the log before they went into the vault.

Maybe I could volunteer.

As for the email…

I clicked *Yes*. Yes, I was crazy. No, I didn't want the evidence sitting in my drafts folder, proving to everyone that I'd gone straight screaming around the bend.

I wasn't tired at all. I felt as if I'd slept for hours. I put clean clothes on and slipped my phone into my pocket.

The cat followed me out of the room. It seemed to approve.

Meritre would have said that was an omen. Who was I to say she was wrong?

# Meru

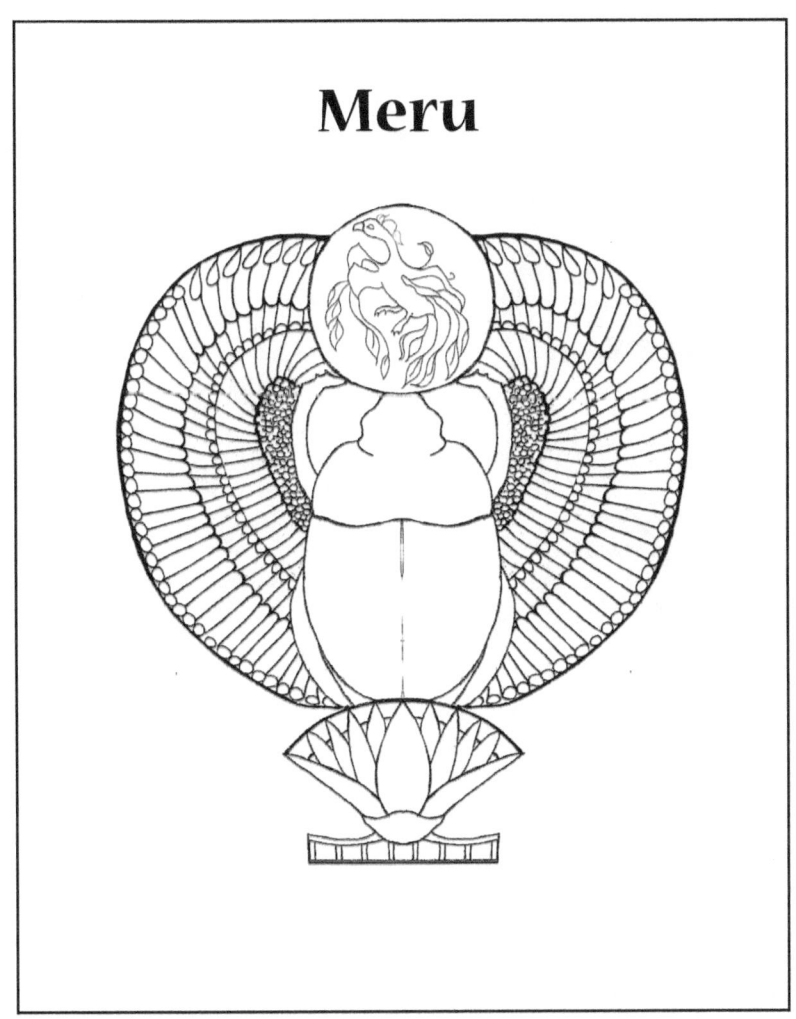

# Chapter 12

Containment was a bare and echoing cavern of a hall divided by force fields into a maze of rooms and cells. The fields in the cells were opaque, like walls of shimmering steel; they cut off sound as well as sight. Only the front wall was transparent.

Meru's cell was one of the first. She could see the Guards leading new prisoners past her, as ruffled and wide-eyed from decontamination as she had been, but most were much less quiet.

She was careful not to look up. The starwing had gone invisible, but she could feel it near the summit of the vault. It watched over her as always; its calm flowed through her. She was safe—bored, twitching at the separation from the web, but safe.

She had tried already to reboot the web with the backup chip she had brought from home. She pressed it into her ear under cover of lying down to rest, and felt it click into the port inside the canal. Then she waited, but nothing happened.

The chip worked: it sent her the right messages as it logged into her neural network. But when it tried to connect to the web, it failed.

She pushed herself back to her feet. Even with the starwing to take the edge off, she was ready to fly apart.

There was water in the cell, and an elegant little box of sweet bean buns and pickled vegetables and groundnut soup that told her Vekaa had ordered it: it was exactly as she liked it, as if it had come from the family's kitchen. That made her eyes sting.

She had seen Jian dead in front of her, and she had not shed a tear. One cup of starfruit tea with just the right measure of sweetener, and she burst out bawling.

Grief had a way of slipping sideways. Jian had told her that.

Her mother had told her so much. Even spending most of her time off Earth, leaving Meru with the family, she had been there on the web. All Meru had to do was think of her, and even if she was somewhere far and strange, there would be a message or a link or a memory.

Now there was nothing. Jian was gone. No more messages. No more links. Memory should still be there, but all Meru could see was Jian lying dead in that bare and dusty room.

Meru slammed shut the food-storage box without touching anything inside it. Her mouth was dry, but the thought of water made her gag. She paced the floor, not caring how close she came to the wall, even when it stung her.

The pain was welcome. It convinced her that she was real; that even without the web, she could still feel. But when she caught herself standing in the middle of the cell, poised to fling herself headfirst at the shimmer of the field, she stopped short and let her knees go, dropping to the floor.

The floors she had always known gave when a person fell on them. This shocked her with bruises.

That pain on top of the other cleared her head. She could think, more or less. She could focus on something other than her grief, and remember lessons she had learned long ago when she was small, about how the web worked. She still had her implants, complete with backup, and the web was still there. The wall that cut her off was like the force field: it was too strong for a single human to break, but it was not unbreakable.

The starwing had taught her something when it passed through the field around the old city. Brute force was no use. For this kind of work, she had to be subtle. If she could make her virtual self as insubstantial as a starwing, maybe she could penetrate the barrier.

If she did that, she would break laws that had held her world together for hundreds of years. She risked spending the rest of her life in just such a prison as this, cut off from the web without hope of ever finding it again.

They would take her implants, blind and deafen her to the web forever, and make sure she did not die of it. She shuddered on the hard, cold floor.

The starwing stirred on its perch high above her. Its wings spread beyond reach of mere glass and steel.

When Meru looked at them from that angle, they looked strikingly like a neural net. Almost automatically she opened a link through it as if it had been a real net—and it worked. She was so startled she almost fell out of the link, but at the last instant she held on.

The connection was dim and somewhat blurred, but clear enough that she could piece the bits of data together. She scanned the web quickly, braced for the connection to disappear at any moment.

"Meru?"

As grainy and crackly and out of focus as the voice and image were, she still recognized Yoshi.

"Meru! Where are you? What happened?"

Meru's first impulse was to shut him off. But then she realized what his presence meant.

"Yoshi! Can you link me to the feed? Search Northam Starport, old city."

She could feel Yoshi's puzzlement rippling through the interface, and the questions crowding behind it. But all he said was, "There's nothing— Wait. Here."

He sent it to her in a quick burst, blessedly clear but damnably vague, buried in the middle of a news feed: *Northam Starport closed until further notice.*

"That's all I can find," Yoshi said. "Is it unusual? They close SudAfrique every so often, if something alien comes in that might not be safe."

"Something alien," said Meru. "Maybe. Like infection."

"Disease? From offworld?" Yoshi peered at her. "Meru! Are you sick?"

"I am not sick," Meru said. "I am in Containment. I was in the old city. People—people were dead."

"That's not possible. There can't be sickness on Earth. We're protected."

Meru held herself together with teeth-gritted care. "Yoshi, will you let people know I'm alive? And that I'm well?"

"Done," he said with hardly a pause. Then: "Containment? But that's not supposed to be—"

"No, it's not." The connection was starting to fray. "Yoshi! Can you lock in? Not the...usual way."

Not the legal way, she meant. His understanding washed over her, prickling with static.

His link was like a line cast on the tide. Wind and spray tried to catch it and blow it away. Meru lunged for it, and nearly lost that other connection, the one the starwing held.

She hung between the two, with the parts of her virtual self beginning to stretch and fray.

Yoshi reinforced the link with a hack she had never seen before. She wondered if he had, either. A nanosecond later, the starwing sent a surge of energy along it, locking it in place.

It was still very thin and fragile, and it was weak: what data could come through it came in drips and spurts.

"If anything about this comes through," she said to Yoshi, "anywhere, at any time—"

"I'll ping," he said.

She sent a spark of gratitude. He slipped away, but the link held, a tiny, tiny gap in the firewall that barred her from the web.

She explored the edges of the wall, searching for any other crack or weakness. But unlike the force field around the old city, this virtual barrier was new and fresh and strong.

After what seemed a very long time, in a far, far corner, she found a glimmer of light. It was even stranger than the link to Yoshi: without discernible source, and clear in all dimensions, even taste and smell, but weirdly remote. In one way she was part of it, as if she were the one walking down the odd square corridor past rows of closed doors. In another, she watched from above, like a starwing.

In that strange doubling of senses, she understood that she, or rather the persona on the web, was looking for something. There was a sense of age around that unspecified thing, a taste of sun and sand, and a sense that it had something to do with sickness and dying, and a mother's face.

Meru must have fallen into one of the endless games that ran across the web, some so old that no one remembered where or when they began. She found them dull and usually shut them off. When she could spare any time to play, she played at being a starpilot, sailing across the sea of stars.

This game for all its antique simplicity was oddly compelling. When the persona opened one of the doors—a thing so ancient it turned on hinges— and found herself in a high dim room full of shelves and boxes, Meru felt the same excitement and the same stab of guilty fear as the player, whoever it was, who ran the game.

The room had a distinct smell, sharp as a sneeze, like dust and ancient spices. At the far end was the steel door of the vault, locked and sealed.

Everything outside it was either the archive—paper and printout: this game was truly ancient—or artifacts that were being studied or were not yet catalogued.

She was the only person in the room. Whoever had left the door unlocked would get in trouble for it, the persona suspected, then felt guilty all over again for being glad that someone had made a mistake.

She had to move fast. There was no telling when one of the students would come back. She scanned the room, trying to focus, to find one particular box in a room full of them. Her mind kept skipping over the numbers she had seen written on the box.

She stopped and took a deep breath. The box had come in today. No one had had time to do any archiving or filing. It had to be close to the door.

There—on the table labeled, of course, *New Finds*. The persona laughed at herself, breathed deep again, and lifted the lid from the box that sat on top of the rest.

It was full of beads or carved stones, most of them blue or green; a great many were identical. The persona looked at them in a wave of despair. How was she supposed to know which was the one she needed?

Meru could answer that. In games like this, the talisman had a marker on it, a tiny spurt of data that signaled when it was found.

The persona started slightly. Had it felt Meru's presence? Its hand passed over the rows of stones.

Meru felt it when the persona did: not exactly like the crackle of a data spurt, but close enough. One blue stone, domed on the top, flat on the bottom, carved in the rough image of a beetle, was the one.

The persona lifted it out of the box. It had a hole through it, as a bead should. One like it hung around the persona's neck.

As far as Meru could tell, the two beads were identical, except that the one from the box was older. Much older.

It lay in the persona's trembling palm. Short pale fingers closed over it. Guilt rose and crested. This was stealing. And yet—if it did what it was supposed to, if it could help—

"Meru."

Vekaa's voice wrenched her out of the game. That was all the more shocking because it should not have happened. A person had to log out and shut down in order to leave a game, even when someone pinged from outside. This was like being roused abruptly from a dream.

Meru lay on the floor of the cell, blinking at her uncle. She must have fallen asleep. Of course she would dream of the web, since for the first time in her life she was cut off from it.

The dream refused to let go. She stared at Vekaa through it, sitting up groggily. While she dreamed or played the game or whatever she had done, memory of her mother had slipped away. Vekaa's face brought it back.

He looked as empty as she felt. It was not kind of her, but she was glad. "I'm sorry," he said, "for everything I've done to you and everything I'm going to have to do. I can't let you out of this building and I can't let you go home. I can't even send someone to keep you company. But I can move you to a more comfortable room."

Meru reached for the web instinctively, and flinched when she met the wall. Yoshi's link was still there, but it seemed even thinner than before. She dared not send any data down it, or hope to get anything back.

She had to ask Vekaa a question that no one asked any more, because the answer was instant, woven into on the web: "How long has it been?"

"It's morning," he said. "You've been here all night. I'm sorry for that, too. Once the disease is fully contained, we can unlock the web, but until then—"

"You don't want to panic people," Meru said. "I understand. Can you at least tell me when you think it will be over? It must be contained by now, or nearly."

His face tightened. "It's been…unusually resistant."

"I'm not sick," Meru said. "I was decontaminated. You're in here with me, so I mustn't be a risk of infection. If I swear not to tell anyone what's happening, even—even what happened to Jian, will you let me go home?"

She got that out without breaking down. She was proud of herself.

Vekaa had gone stiff. His voice when he spoke was cold, as if they were strangers. "We can't do that. We're all on lockdown until we know what it is and how it mutates. We're not even sure that once everything is decontaminated, it won't come back."

Meru knew why he did that. He belonged to Consensus, and Consensus had to make its decisions for everyone, not just for one person. He must be hurting terribly inside.

But it hurt her, too. "I understand," she said. "I do. But—"

"Then you understand that we have to consider all the possibilities," Vekaa said. He held out his hand. "I promise I won't let them keep you for one moment longer than they absolutely have to."

Meru let him pull her to her feet. He would have held on, maybe to comfort her, maybe himself, but she slipped free.

She heard his faint sigh. Meru had always been prickly and fiercely independent. Neither was a virtue.

She got both from her mother. A wave of grief struck her, so strong she could hardly stand up.

She stiffened her knees and made her face as still as she could. Vekaa had not seen: he had stepped outside the cell and stood waiting for her to follow.

She braced as she passed the doorway, but the field was down. It was kind of Vekaa to trust her, and not surround her with Guards.

Vekaa knew as well as she did that there was no way out of here, unless the starwing could find one. At the moment Meru was not ready to ask. She wanted to escape, but she needed to know more.

There were things Vekaa was not saying. If she stayed, she might learn what they were.

Curiosity was a starpilot's virtue, if not an Earthling's. It also gave Meru something focus on. She followed her uncle out of the cells into a physical space so much like the web that she stopped, caught off balance.

The web was still out of her reach. But the heart of Containment was its own network of interlocking data streams. Where the web was all internal, this was actually visible: a enormous sphere interlaced with the glimmering ribbons of walkways, through which people moved, tracking the streams of data that were there already and building new ones with speed and skill that told her just how serious this crisis was.

Plagues and epidemics had always seemed remote to her, like stories of things that happened offworld, to other people. Meru studied them because her mother did, and because she was going to live off Earth; she had to know what they were like. But she never really, deeply felt any of them. She was sad, she pitied the people who were sick or died, then another tragedy swam up through the data streams and she forgot about it.

This was happening to Meru. It was real and strong and immediate. It had killed her mother.

Vekaa had stopped walking along the ribbon that led up from the cells to the center of the sphere, and turned to face her. Someone else had come from above to stand beside him, a woman Meru had never met but knew well from the web.

Her name was Lyra. She was a Decider. When decisions had to be made on Earth, Lyra was one of those who made them.

If she was here, this was more than serious. Meru could think of nothing to say, could only stand and stare.

Lyra smiled, which did not put Meru at ease at all. "We are most sorry for your loss," she said. She sounded as if she meant it, though she moved on quickly, as if her duty was done and now she could get back to what really concerned her. "We hope you don't mind that I've ordered breakfast for us."

It would have made no difference if Meru had minded. She made herself nod and say something suitably grateful. Her stomach had clenched and would not let go.

Breakfast waited on the edge of the sphere, high up on the side opposite the cells, in a bubble that seemed to float under the sea. Bright fish swam all around it; now and then through the watery silence came the song of a whale.

This was meant to be a refuge, an island of peace. Meru had no peace in her. She did not think she ever would again.

In spite of everything, she was ravenously hungry. She only realized that the others were barely picking at their food as she reached for the third kelp roll. They were waiting for her to finish eating.

She set the roll down uneaten and folded her hands in her lap. The knot in her stomach had come back; the food she had gulped down only made it worse.

Lyra glanced at Vekaa and nodded slightly. He closed his eyes, then opened them, and reached under the table, drawing out a package wrapped in shimmering fabric. He slid it across the table toward Meru.

She made no move to take it. "What is this?"

"Your mother left it," he said. "It's keyed to you."

Her hands twitched, but she held them still. She could see the seal on the package, with another over it, declaring it decontaminated.

She was not afraid of catching the plague. Something else made her hesitate. Both of the others were trying hard to seem calm, but the tension was so strong she could taste it.

"We believe," Lyra said when it was clear that Meru was not going to move, "that your mother knew something of what was happening here. She broke off an expedition that had been years in the planning, talked her way onto the first ship that would take her within jump distance of this system, and came on-world under diplomatic cover. She left no records, no clues as to why—only this."

Meru would not be angry. She would *not*. "My mother was an interstellar spy?"

Vekaa bit his lip. Meru could not tell whether he wanted to laugh or cry.

Lyra was in better control of herself. Of course she would be. Jian had been nothing to her but a name.

That made Meru angry, too, but not so angry that she missed what Lyra was saying. "We don't think she was a spy," the Decider said. "Some of what she did might have skirted the edges of local authority, but she was always careful to stay on the side of the law. She was following the path of a particular colonial expansion, outward from Earth to worlds that were uninhabited when the colonists came to them."

"Some of those worlds had had intelligent life," said Vekaa, "but it was long gone."

"Plague?" Meru asked.

He nodded. He was steadier now that he could be a scientist and not a brother. "That was her specialty, after all: the effect of epidemics on starfaring cultures. We're looking for patterns in the research she did, but so far we haven't found any that would lead her to Earth. Maybe she left something in that package."

Meru understood his meaning perfectly. If it was keyed to her, nothing and no one else could open it.

They were desperate for answers. So was she. But she was—not afraid, no, but uncertain. What if the answer was something none of them could bear to know?

People were dying. Jian was dead. What could be worse than that?

Slowly Meru drew the package toward her. She took a deep breath and tried not to shake. When she touched the seal, the wrapping folded back. Inside was a packet in a crackly brownish wrapper, with words written on it in ancient ink: *This is the key.*

Something was rolled up inside, tumbling out onto the table. Meru stared blankly at the thing her mother had left her.

It was a stasis field; it contained a withered flower and a blue bead. She had seen a bead exactly like it, and held it in her hand, during the game that she had thought was a dream.

# Meredith

# Chapter 13

I had the scarab in my hand. I could put it back and walk away and avoid stealing it, and keep out of trouble. I could just sit there and let the world spin down the drain, too, taking everybody with it.

Or I could borrow it. All right, steal it, but I'd put it back when I was done. There were so many in that box, and hundreds more in storage. What difference did it make if one went somewhere else for a while?

I wrapped it in the napkin I'd brought and shoved it in my pocket. Then I got out of there.

I'd never done anything like that in my life. I could feel it in there, as if it was literally hot. Any minute I expected alarms to go off and buzzers to buzz and Aunt Jessie to leap out of a cupboard chanting *Thief! Thief! Thief!*

The silence was almost worse. Somehow, before it broke and I got busted, I had to figure out how to get to the marketplace, bazaar, whatever they called it.

People would expect me to want to play tourist, at least I hoped so. I also hoped they wouldn't ask too many questions about what I wanted to buy.

Some of it maybe wasn't legal. Then there was the question I really needed to ask. Does magic work if you don't believe in it?

I was afraid I already knew the answer to that.

Everything's on the internet somewhere, and normally that's the first place I would have gone to look. But artifact storage was right above the library, and I was going by the door when the questions started crowding in. Instead of diving for my room and my computer, I went really old school. Ancient. I dived for the books.

So many of them were in languages I didn't know. The ones that were in English were all tangled up in their own words. I was ready to give up and head for the beautiful, simple, searchable internet when I found the box at the end of the shelf.

The label on it was typed, and so old it had gone yellow and started to peel. All it said was, *Misc. Notes on Magical Texts*.

Why not? I thought, pulling it out and lugging it to the table I'd staked out at the end of the aisle under the window.

The box was full of hand-written notes. There were sheets of hieroglyphs, drawn and painted with care that must have taken hours, and then there were the translations. They were scribbled and crossed out and rewritten all over the place, but they surprised me by being easy to read. Whoever wrote them—I couldn't find a name anywhere—had round, clear handwriting. It was as careful, in its way, as the hieroglyphs.

Nobody writes like that any more. I was glad this person had, whoever he or she was, because when I started to piece it together, I realized what I was reading. It was Meritre's book of magic.

I don't believe in coincidences, either. My hands shook when I spread the pages across the table.

There it was, the spell Meritre was going to—had intended to—must have gone ahead and worked.

This time-traveling thing was making my head ache.

There it was, anyway. It was a recipe for wiping out evil. It called for a crocodile's egg, crushed beetles' wings, a jug of beer, and the dung of a white cow.

I pulled out my phone and took a picture of the translation. Then I took a picture of the original. And after that I snapped bits of the rest, more or less at random, until I stopped short.

"This is stupid," I said.

I'd been thinking about how to make the spell work. Egypt isn't ancient any more. Food has changed, though not as much as you might think. Spells might change, too.

I could get an egg, though it probably wouldn't be a crocodile's. Beetles were all over the place. Beer, no problem, though I'd have to sneak it out of the kitchen. The cow…well…

It *was* stupid. All the spell did was make the world's worst plate of scrambled eggs.

I shuffled the papers together and dropped them back in the box. Just after it slid into its place on the shelf, Aunt Jessie opened the library door and squinted down the aisle. "Meredith, is that you?"

"Coming," I said. "Sorry, did you lose me? I just couldn't resist—"

"Of course you couldn't."

I held my breath, but it seemed I didn't have either *Thief* or *Liar* painted on my forehead.

Aunt Jessie wasn't really looking at me. She had an odd expression on her face. "You have visitors," she said.

Now that *was* odd. Who in the world…?

---

Who's the world traveler in the family?

Dad was waiting for me in the lounge outside the dining commons. It had a lot of leather chairs and couches and bookshelves full of anything and everything, a piano that Jonathan had told me belonged to Howard Carter— the man himself, the one who found King Tut's tomb—and a television set so old it didn't even have a remote, and a sound system so new I wasn't sure if some of its components had been invented yet.

I wasn't at all surprised to find Dad fiddling with the sound system. He had it playing a funky mix of Beatles songs, which was a totally Dad thing to do.

I love my Dad. When he can be bothered to be around, he's more fun than anybody I know. He's been everywhere and done everything, and there isn't anything he isn't interested in.

Mom used to be like him, everybody tells me. By the time Dad bought the sailing schooner and started running charter cruises out of Key West, I'd come along and Mom was 'way over her experimental phase. She bought the house on the mainland and joined the law firm, and Dad stopped by in between cruises.

The visits got further and further apart. By the time I taught myself to read, one of the first things I figured out was a postcard from Dad from the Bering Sea. He'd signed on for a season on a crab boat, then he was headed to Mongolia to run a trekking company. Ponies on the steppe, nights in a yurt—every horse kid's dream.

That's how I got into horses. I was determined to learn to ride and then go and help Dad with his company. Dad moved on; he always did. I stayed with the horses, and Florida, and Mom.

The last I heard, he was in India doing something high-tech. Or training elephants; his messages weren't too clear. Now here he was in Luxor, looking just the same as always, long and tall and sunburned.

He didn't have a beard this round, and he'd cut his hair. I liked him that way. His bright blue eyes hadn't changed even slightly, or the wide white grin. He picked me up and hugged me so tight my ribs creaked.

I was getting old for that, but just before I started to go stiff, he put me down. "Fancy meeting you here," he said.

"That was *my* line," I said. "What are you doing here? Aren't you supposed to be in an ashram or something?"

"That was last year." I couldn't tell if he was laughing at me or not. "I just got off a Greenpeace cruise in the Indian Ocean. Since I was so close, relatively speaking, I thought I'd stop by and see how you're doing."

I narrowed my eyes at him. Dad would think like that, for sure, but he never had just one thing going on.

"If you're not too tired," he said, "I'd like to take you to dinner. You up for it?"

I glanced at Aunt Jessie. She wouldn't hesitate to tell either of us if she thought he was full of it, but she spread her hands. "Up to you," she said.

I was tired and jetlagged and I had more on my mind than a sane person ought to have, but if Dad was up to something, I wanted to know it now instead of days or weeks from now. "All right," I said. "I'll go get changed."

Trust Dad to stay in a hotel that looked as if you'd find Indiana Jones in the next room, or the kind of lady archaeologist who'd stow a sword inside her parasol. It had actual, modern air conditioning, but the big ceiling fans were still there and still turning, and the dining room was full of potted palms and people in khaki. There was at least one busload of German tourists, and the British accents were out in force.

The waiter was a disappointment. They wear the same uniform in Florida, white shirt and black pants. The fact he was drop-dead cute about halfway made up for it.

The table he took us to had someone sitting at it. She was tall and narrow like Dad, with short blonde hair and serious cheekbones.

I'd kill for those cheekbones. I could see her in a long white dress and a parasol, though what she had on was a light green sundress and clunky sandals.

The sandals made me like her in spite of the cheekbones. "Meredith," Dad said with a funny little upward tilt in his voice, "this is Kelly."

I'd expected her to be called Ute or Gretchen. She stood up and shook my hand and said in perfectly normal American, "Hello, Meredith. I've heard a lot about you."

I couldn't say the same. I smiled and said polite things, and waited for Dad to explain.

Dad didn't take off because he was sick of Mom. He just couldn't stay in one place for more than a few months at a time before his feet got so itchy he couldn't stand it. It was Mom who filed for divorce.

I'd been expecting him to show up with someone else eventually, but it never quite got around to happening, and I'd got used to things being the way they were. This caught me completely off guard. I sat down because it was better than falling down, and ordered something, I hardly noticed what.

Dad and Kelly were sitting carefully apart, not holding hands or kissing or doing anything that might be expected to upset me. It was too careful; they would barely even look at each other. They were trying too hard. That just made it more awkward.

The explanation was no surprise. "We met on the Greenpeace cruise," Kelly said, "then we took off on our own for an eco-tour of the Indian Ocean. Now I'm headed back to Chicago, and Mark's decided to come with me."

She smiled at him, not sappy at all, and then turned back to me. She had a way of looking at a person straight on that made me feel as if I really did matter to her—not because she felt obligated to be nice to the boyfriend's kid, but because I was a human being, and she was interested in who and what I was.

She was good. She didn't even make me want to hate her.

I could see why Dad liked her so much. What I couldn't see was him going anywhere for someone else. "Chicago?" I said.

I must have sounded totally shocked, because Dad laughed. "Why not?" he said. "It's a great city. Lots going on. Plenty of water, even, in Lake Michigan, if I get the urge to go out in a boat again."

"What will you do?" I asked.

"I've got a job doing tech support for the main office of the eco-tours company," he said. "It's right near the hospital where Kelly is finishing up her residency, so it's all working out."

My eyebrows went up. "You're a doctor?" I said.

Kelly nodded. "One more year," she said, "then I'm loose upon the world."

"Let me guess," I said. "Doctors Without Borders."

She had a great smile, wide and a little crooked. "Eventually. There's so much work to do inside the country, right in Chicago. I'll start there and see where it takes me."

It's hard to know what to say when you're a normal selfish human and the person you're talking to is a saint. Lucky for me, our salads came right then, and we were too busy eating to talk much.

Dad dropped the other half of the bomb in the middle of dessert. "We'll be here for a few days," he said, "then we're off to Florida."

I sat with my spoonful of crème brûlée halfway to my mouth. "I thought you said Chicago."

"We'll end up in Chicago," he said. "We're stopping to see your mother first."

I lowered the spoon into the bowl. "Does she know that?"

"I talked to her," said Dad. "I told her about Kelly; they're anxious to meet each other."

"When did you do that?"

"A couple of days ago," Dad said.

I bit my lip. Mom hadn't told Dad about the cancer. She didn't want him fluttering around her, as she put it. Now she was in remission, I guess she figured it was all right.

And here was Dad coming to visit with his girlfriend the doctor.

Sometimes things do just happen.

True. And sometimes they don't.

I picked at what was left of the brûlée now I'd eaten most of the crème from underneath it, making it pop and crackle. "What kind of doctor are you?" I asked.

Dad and Kelly looked at each other. He'd stopped smiling.

Kelly looked away a little too quickly, straight at me. "I'm an oncologist," she said. "A cancer specialist."

"Of course you are."

That slipped out. I didn't mean for anyone to think Dad would get interested in somebody just so he could get free medical advice. It just happened that this really cool, really unspeakably *nice* person would know exactly what she was looking at the minute she met Mom.

Mom had to know. She could get your entire life history in the first five minutes after she met you, on the phone or off.

If she wasn't worried, I shouldn't be, either. That didn't stop me. "You know," I said.

Dad nodded. The way he breathed in and then out, I knew he'd been holding his breath.

"All along?"

He nodded again. "She asked me not to come," he said. "Then she went into remission. So it all came out right in the end."

"But now?"

"We're just stopping to visit," he said. "I do that every few years. We're still friends. You know that."

I did know it. I also knew that if I were Dad, it would be just like me to want Mom to meet the new girlfriend. I might not break up with her if Mom didn't like her, but it would matter. Mom mattered.

I pushed the long-dead bowl of crème brûlée away. I don't know why I felt like crying. "I'd like to go back to the house now," I said, "if you don't mind."

They didn't mind at all. They were probably as glad to drop me off at Luxor House as I was to escape.

I couldn't escape myself. My other selves, or whatever they were—I couldn't get away from them, either. Asleep or awake, wherever I looked, there I was.

# Meredith

# Chapter 14

As soon as the sun sprang into the sky, Meritre knew that she had dreamed true. The plague had come back in the night and seized the king's daughter.

When Meritre and her mother came to the temple in the morning, the mistress of the chorus stood with the high priest and a man in a massive wig and a collar of honor so heavy with gold that it bowed his narrow shoulders. "The king needs your voices," he said.

All of the singers bowed to the king's will. Neither the hymn nor the festival of the plague's ending would matter if the king's daughter died.

Meritre had never been inside the palace before. She had seen it from the outside, of course, and she had seen the king in the temple or passing in procession through the streets, carried high on the shoulders of strong men. The sheen of divinity surrounded her; her face was a painted mask beneath the lofty height of the double crown. Because she was king, she wore the false beard strapped to her chin, and carried her head high with her eyes fixed far above mere mortal things.

Led by the king's messenger, the singers went by ways that must be familiar to servants, past the palace wall into a maze of courts and corridors. They were not all wide, high, or splendidly ornamented; some, except for the length and the elaborateness of the painted walls, might have belonged to any ordinary house. Meritre had half expected the floors to be paved with gold, but those inside were tiled in colors that matched the walls, red and white and green and blue, and the pavements outside were broad smoothed stones, just as in the temple.

She had heard that people who came to the palace had to wait, sometimes for days, until the royal personage would deign to see them. That would be difficult, she thought, with Father and the boys—and what of Djehuti? How could she work the spell she meant to work, if she was trapped in the palace?

She shut off that thought before it made her do anything foolish. The queen's messenger walked so fast that Meritre was breathless, which helped to distract her. So did her mother, who neither faltered nor complained, but her face had a still, set look that Meritre did not like.

Just as Meritre made up her mind to call on their guide to slow down, he stopped. The door in front of him boasted a pair of guards with tall spears.

Beyond the door was, at last, the sort of place that Meritre imagined when she thought of palaces. Tall golden columns marched around the edges of a courtyard bursting with greenery and wild with flowers. In the center gleamed a pool, mirroring the clear blue of the sky.

Beside the pool, shaded by a gold-embroidered canopy, lay a bed supported on backs of carved and gilded falcons with their wings outspread. The figure that lay on it seemed terribly small and slight.

A crowd of people surrounded the bed, but Meritre saw only one: a woman in a plain linen gown and simple wig, who sat on a stool and held the princess' hand. She could have been a nurse or a servant, but the way the people around her stood, giving her more space than they gave anyone else, told Meritre she was more than that.

One glance, one turn of that deceptively humble head, and the crowd all but disappeared. A handful of women stayed, doing useful things: fanning the princess, moistening her cracked lips with water and sweet oil, bathing her body with cool cloths. For the racking coughs they could do nothing, except pray.

The king turned her gaze on the singers from the temple. Her eyes were long and dark, painted with kohl and malachite as everyone's eyes were. Her face was neither beautiful nor ugly. She could have been anyone: a servant, a shopkeeper, a sculptor's wife. And yet there was no doubt in the world that she was the king.

"The gods are not listening to me," she said. Her voice was low and clear; unlike her face, it was beautiful. "Maybe they will hear you. Sing for her. Pray to the gods that she may live."

The singers glanced at one another. Aweret had recovered from the speed of her arrival: she stood straight, breathing only a little quickly. She raised her chin and sang the first pure note of the hymn to Isis, mother and healer.

Meritre caught the note and carried it. One by one the rest followed.

In this garden of the palace, with so many green things growing and breathing around them, the quality of the hymn was distinctly different than in the stone court of the temple. Parts of it were softer, sinking into the leaves and the water. Parts rose even higher and clearer. They surrounded the princess with a web of sweet sound.

As the choir of Amon sang, the king ordered sacrifices in every temple and prayer in every house and palace. The princess' name would be on every tongue in Egypt, and every worker of magic, from the greatest to the least, was commanded to call up his power.

As hymn after hymn flowed through Meritre's throat, her ears and mind recorded the king's words and her commands. She was storming heaven, raising every force she had against the gods, while physicians jostled sorcerers at the princess' bedside. This was her heir, her beloved. She must live. She must not die.

That was a mother's love for her child. It was fierce; it knew no reason.

Meritre had no child yet, but she loved her mother. She had loved her sister Iry, whom the plague had taken. She could understand, at least a little.

She sang the hymns and prayers with all her heart. She did her best to hope. But even in the bright sunlight, shadows crowded close.

In her heart she saw the princess dead on a bier, and the king bowed down in mourning. She saw the plague ended at last, gone away out of Egypt, now that it had taken that final sacrifice.

It was as clear as the sunlight that she saw every day, the streets she lived in and the temple in which she served. She saw grief, and she saw hope. She saw so much of everything that was or would be that it surged up over her and drowned her.

The hymn had ended, but no one had moved to begin another. The sun was much lower than it had been when Meritre last looked.

The princess tossed in her fever dream. Her breathing had thickened; there was a rattle in it.

Meritre knew that sound. So did anyone who was still alive in this part of the world. That was death closing the doors of the lungs.

"There is no hope?" the king demanded. "None whatever?"

Her eyes were on Meritre. The force of her desperation was like a hot wind out of the desert, blowing from the land of the dead.

Meritre must have spoken her visions aloud. She felt cold and sick inside. Still, the king had asked a question. She had to answer. "There is always hope," she said. Her voice shook a little, because she was mortal and this was a goddess on Earth. "This is the end; the plague is gone. It will be long years before Egypt suffers another."

"You know this?" said the king.

Meritre would happily have crawled into a hole at the foot of the nearest palm tree, but now she had begun, she had to finish. "I see it. The gods make you a promise: once this price is paid and this sacrifice made, there will be no more while you live."

"What if I refuse?" the king said. "What if I will not give her up?"

Meritre set her lips together. There was no answer she could give that would not enrage the king. Silence would not please her, either, but it might be a fraction less dangerous.

The king bent over her daughter. The child still breathed, but the rattle was louder. Her face was grey and sunken, as if death had already taken her.

There were no hymns left to sing that would not seem to mock the king's grief. It hardly mattered. If the gods were listening, none was inclined to answer.

The sun hung just above the wall. A breath of wind played through the garden, ruffling the fronds of the palms and making the flowers sway. Meritre breathed in their sweetness.

She braced for another vision, but nothing came to her except fragments that made no sense: a white animal like a huge dog or an impossibly strange and gigantic gazelle; a broken wall beneath a sky full of stars; a shadow with wings.

The king's sorcerers raised their smokes and stinks and chanted their spells. With a small but potent shock, Meritre recognized the one she had been going to try with Djehuti.

It was not nearly as impressive as she had hoped. Her hand rose to the amulet that hung around her neck. For an instant it felt strange, as if it had come alive. But when she touched it, it was the same as always.

The princess' breathing stopped. So, for a long count of heartbeats, did the wind.

One of the maids began to wail. The others took up the chorus, with the priests and sorcerers, and even a handful of the temple singers.

Meritre had no voice left. Nor, it seemed, did Aweret, or the king.

Aweret's knees gave way. Meritre went down with her to the smooth warmth of the paving. Aweret's eyes were open; she was conscious, but the strength had run out of her.

No one cared for one commoner among the silenced chorus. There was water in a jar near enough for Meritre to reach, with a dipper beside it. Probably she should beg someone's leave, but who would listen?

She dipped a ladleful and coaxed it into Aweret. It seemed to help a little. Aweret sighed and leaned her head against Meritre's shoulder.

Everyone else was lost to reason. People ran without sense or direction, shrilling and keening.

The king did nothing to stop or direct them. She sat on her stool with the princess' hand still in hers. For her, the world had stopped.

The king was a god and Meritre most surely was not, but that deep and terrible stillness she did understand. That was death, which was stronger than gods.

The sun set on them all, leaving them in twilight rent with weeping, as word of the plague's last victim spread through the city. The singers of Amon stayed in the garden, hungry and thirsty, until a servant who was both wise and kind brought them bread and beer and a basket of dates.

Meritre made sure that her mother had a fair share. Aweret ate slowly and without appetite, but she was wise enough to know that she had to keep herself and the baby fed.

At last one of the priests found the presence of mind to dismiss the singers. They left gratefully, making their way through a palace in uproar and a city that seemed unlikely to sleep tonight.

When hundreds of common people and even nobles died, there had been mourning enough. Now that the king's heir was dead, the world's foundations were shaken. The best Meritre could think of to do was get her mother home, hope Father and the boys had managed to feed themselves, and then hope any of them could manage to rest.

It was slow going. Torches blazed on roofs and in doorways. The streets were full of people who had let go all restraint. All the grief, all the anger and sorrow that the plague had brought, burst out on this terrible night.

Meritre clung to the edges as much as she could, shielded Aweret with her body and held firm against jostling and outright blows. Someone's elbow caught her lip and split it; before she was halfway home, she was covered in lesser bruises. But Aweret was safe, and that was all that mattered.

The market near their house had closed before sunset, but it was full of people. The air reeked of beer. Meritre set her teeth, held tight to Aweret, and dived into the crowd.

She rocked like a boat in a flood. Her mother's arms were firm around her, as if somehow she had found new strength. It would not last, but it might get them through this last and worst ordeal before they were safe inside their own walls.

A mob of men lurched past in a haze of beer. They knocked Meritre half off her feet and sent her staggering against a shuttered booth. Someone else was there already; he grunted as Meritre collided with him, and staggered back but did not fall.

She looked up startled in the fitful torchlight, into Djehuti's face. He looked less surprised than she: he must have seen her coming. "You waited all this time?" she said, forgetting for an instant that her mother was between them.

"It seemed safer than trying to leave," he said. He sounded the same as always, calm and unruffled, though his cheek was dark with bruising and his kilt was torn.

"Come home with us," Aweret said, too tired or too wise to ask questions. "The sooner we're all in the house, the better we'll be."

Meritre agreed with that wholeheartedly. So did Djehuti. With Aweret between them, doubly safe now, they braved the torrent of people for one last time.

# Meredith

# Chapter 15

Dad stayed longer than I thought he would. A week after he showed up at Luxor House, he was still in town. He and Kelly were doing tours of all the greatest hits. On Friday, which is the Muslim Sunday so everyone has the day off, Aunt Jessie got us into King Tut's tomb and we got to stay for as long as the heat would let us.

It wasn't till after that that he and Kelly made it to Aunt Jessie's dig. I was still on shard-and-scarab duty. I was getting good at it, maybe too good: nobody would want me down in the trenches, where things were getting frustrating and Aunt Jessie was about to give up on the latest tunnel and try somewhere else.

I kept trying to find ways to get through to Meru or Meritre when I wanted to, and not just at random. Nothing worked. I wasn't dreaming about them, either, but small things kept me from thinking I'd imagined the whole thing. I'd smell beer or feel the starwing close by, or look up and for a split second the daylight sky would be full of stars.

They were still there, just not on top. When I did dream, I'd be riding Bonnie through the palmettos to the river, or counting turtle eggs while the moon shone on the ocean. Sometimes I was alone. More often, especially if I'd been Skyping or texting before I went to sleep, the usuals were with me.

Those were peaceful dreams, full of ordinary and comfortable and quietly wonderful things; I'd wake happy. Then during the days I was so busy just being in Egypt that I hardly had time to think about anything else.

That was deliberate. I'd been hearing from everybody as often as I could get a phone signal, and everybody told me everything, especially about Bonnie. But there was never much from Mom. A one-liner once or twice a day, saying thanks for the ten-screen epic I'd sent her, and a couple of texts, that was it. No Skype.

She must be busy. Summer in Florida is crazy season; the heat drives people nuts, then they start shooting at each other. Her court docket would be running over.

Then there was the time difference. She probably meant to call, but kept forgetting how late or how early it would be here.

One of these days she'd get around to sending me her own epic. In the meantime I wasn't going to panic. If anything awful happened, Aunt Jessie would tell me. Wouldn't she?

The day Dad came to the site, I finished labeling my box of shards before the heat got too ridiculous. Gwyn saw me twitching; she smiled and said, "Go on. I'm almost done, too."

I didn't wait for her to change her mind. I grabbed my water bottle and sunglasses and dived out of the tent.

After the first shock, the heat really wasn't bad. It helped to slow down, chart a path from shade to shade, and keep sipping from the bottle.

The crew was working in the tunnel that slanted down off the side of the temple. Aunt Jessie had been playing a hunch, and arguing with her students over it. They said there couldn't be a tomb that close or that obvious. Aunt Jessie kept saying, "Have you ever heard of hiding in plain sight?"

The digging had gone down a good hundred yards, and so far all they were finding was sand, rubble, and a lot of nothing. The first twenty yards or so were painted from floor to ceiling with hieroglyphs, but then those stopped and there was just bare brick, not even covered with plaster.

If they didn't find something today that would encourage them to keep on, they were going to give up and go back to one of the other tunnels. They might even try somewhere new—Hamid had a theory about a cave he'd found up under the ridge.

Things were tense on the site this morning. Dad and Kelly showing up didn't help much. Aunt Jessie left the tunnel to show them around the parts of the temple that were already excavated.

I wasn't supposed to go in the tunnel without someone to babysit, but everybody was either down there, in one of the tents doing the same sorts of things Gwyn and I did, or playing tour guide. I sneaked down a little ways, not so far I needed the lights that were strung up along the ceiling, but far enough that the light outside barely made it. I could hear voices farther down, and scraping and pounding. They must have hit another wall of rubble.

I stopped because I felt weird all of a sudden: not sick exactly, or scared, but not normal, either. It felt like something soft and cold walking down my spine.

The wall paintings stopped just past where I was standing. This was where they'd found the scarab, more or less.

I still had it, wrapped in its napkin; I kept it in my pocket every day and slept with it under my pillow at night. It didn't do anything magical. When I rubbed it or concentrated on it till I gave myself a headache, nothing ever happened.

I couldn't bring myself to sneak it back where it belonged, though guilt dug like a splinter under my skin. My hand was in my pocket now, curled around it, the way it kept doing if I didn't pay attention.

I knelt down and touched the floor with my other hand, and saw the scarab lying there, where it must have rolled down the slight but obvious slope.

The eyes that saw it weren't mine, and neither was the time they lived in. I knew that because when I looked up, the paintings on the walls were bright and new.

They told a story of a king who loved her daughter as much as any mother had ever loved a child. Then the gods demanded a sacrifice, and the king had this temple built, raising it in seventy days while the princess' body lay in its vat, being preserved for eternity.

It wasn't an enormous feat like building Pyramids, but for people without wheels or machines to shape those columns and carve those stones and paint those walls in just over two months, I thought it was impressive. The paint was still damp in the corners when Meritre was there, and in one place it had dripped a little, so the bird with the human head looked as if it was winking at her.

I bent toward that part of the wall. It was worn and faded, but not so much that I couldn't see where the line of black paint had gone a bit crooked.

My skin was all goose-bumpy. Somehow, more than anything else, this made it real. Meritre had been here, in this exact place.

Four thousand years. For most people I know, four years is forever. Before you were born? It might as well be the beginning of the universe.

It was too much. I had to get out of there. I scrambled up and out, toward the line of canvas roofs where all the modern people were.

I heard Aunt Jessie's voice around the corner, inside the main part of the temple. She must be showing Dad the statue they'd dug up, that had them all excited: it showed the king dressed like a woman but wearing the crown and the beard like every other pharaoh.

Then I heard Dad say, "We have to tell her."

"Janet doesn't want that," Aunt Jessie said. She sounded flat, the way I did to myself when I was trying not to scream at somebody. "She wants Meredith to enjoy her time here, and not have to worry."

"She already is worried," Dad said. "She's bottling it up, but it's obvious to me. Don't you think she'd rather know what's going on than get slammed with it as soon as she gets off the plane?"

"There's time enough," Aunt Jessie said. "She deserves not to go crazy because she can't be with her mother."

"What if there isn't time enough? What if she comes home to a funeral? What will that do to her?"

"Mark," Kelly said. I imagined she'd put her hand on his arm, the way Mom would, to calm him down. "You know what the doctors said when I called them. It could be a week, but it could be three months. They'll let us know if anything changes."

"Thank you," Aunt Jessie said with a hint of snap in it, though the snap wasn't for Kelly. "Meanwhile I think it would be a very bad idea to let Meredith know her mother has gone into hospice. We will have to tell her, I'm not arguing with that at all, but let's not do it until we have to."

"I think we have to," Dad said, but Kelly must have given him a look, because he said, "All right. Not today. We do have to talk to her, and the sooner the better. I know Janet talked to you about taking her to Massachusetts after you're done in Egypt, but now I'm moving to Chicago, I'll be set up to have her with me. She'll be a sophomore in the fall, right? So—"

"Junior," Aunt Jessie said. "September birthday. Did you forget? She started high school two years ago."

"Oh," said Dad. "Right. That doesn't change much. There's a great school near where we'll be living, that we can get her into even this late—Kelly's mother is a trustee. The house we're renting is big enough for all of us. We've got it all figured out."

"Have you?" Aunt Jessie said. "Does Janet know that?"

"We're planning to tell her," Dad said. "I don't see how she can argue with it. Meredith will be uprooted no matter what happens. Unless you're moving to Florida?"

Aunt Jessie didn't answer that. I didn't burst in, either, to see what her face said.

The ocean was roaring in my ears. I was cold all over. Inside I felt small and sharp and very, very hard, like a chip of diamond.

Mom had insisted there was nothing wrong. She was still in remission. It was all right for me to be here on the other side of the planet, because she wasn't sick any more. She wasn't going to die.

She lied. She pretended the doctor hadn't found anything in the last checkup, the one in March, right about when I was suddenly getting that surprise birthday present I didn't even want.

He had found something. He'd found death.

Death was all around me here.

I pressed my forehead against the wall. They'd stopped talking around the corner. That was good. I needed the quiet.

A week, Kelly said. She'd said three months, too, but. A week.

Mom was in hospice. People go to hospice to die.

That's why she sent me away. So I wouldn't be there when it happened.

They all knew, and they hadn't told me. They hadn't even hinted.

I wasn't angry yet. They were good, they really were. I'd fallen for the scam.

Oh, I'd guessed, deep down. There was a reason why I didn't want to come to Egypt. But I hadn't let myself admit it. Just that I wanted a nice normal summer with Bonnie and the usuals.

And Mom. Especially Mom.

I went back to the place where the scarab had been. I wasn't trying to time-travel or turn into Meritre or whatever else might be happening. I just needed to be somewhere that Dad and Aunt Jessie weren't.

This time I kept on going down the tunnel. I couldn't hear people working, and nobody was talking. The crew must have quit for the day.

A tiny part of me thought about running back and hiding somewhere more obvious, like the tent I did my work in. I was emphatically not supposed to be down in a tunnel alone with no phone signal and nobody who knew where I'd gone.

The rest of me didn't care. It was cool down here—surprisingly. I thought I'd heard people say it was horribly hot, and the crews needed fans to keep from passing out.

This was like the cave Dad took me to once, where after you got in, the temperature was always the same. The string of lights stretched down ahead of me. It wasn't very bright, so there were a lot of shadows. I couldn't see all that far ahead.

It should have been spooky. It felt weirdly safe.

I needed safe. Something inside of me, some part I couldn't name or describe, was crumbling, bit by bit. When it was done, I'd be completely empty. There wouldn't be anything left of me at all.

I came to the place where the crew had been working, where they'd been picking away at the rubble. I could see why they'd stopped: they seemed to have hit a dead end.

Aunt Jessie would be disappointed. Hamid might get to explore his cave after all.

The end of the tunnel looked like solid rock, but something about it made my eyes go narrow. I picked up a trowel that someone had left.

This was a bad idea. I wasn't cleared to do any digging. I'd picked around a few sites around home; I knew how to dig out a mammoth bone or an arrowhead. I had no business messing with a real archeological dig.

What difference did it make? This was a big fat zero, and so was I.

I went down on my knees and scraped away at the place where the floor met the rock. For rock, it was soft. It flaked like plaster. Very old plaster, with brick underneath.

My heart started to beat harder. I really ought to stop. But I needed to see. I needed to be sure.

It was a clever piece of plasterwork. It looked exactly like sandstone. If I hadn't had this gut feeling, or maybe it was a memory, I'd never have thought to run a trowel down along the floor, and find the place where the plaster gave way.

Someone's shovel had dug in there, but whoever it was had stopped before he realized he was hitting brick and not solid rock. I worked my way carefully along the crack until I found the next one, the one that went up instead of sideways.

I'd found a door. I knew what was on the other side—what had to be there.

The question was, what did I do about it? Did I tell Aunt Jessie? Or did I let it stay?

That wasn't me thinking. That was Meritre. A tomb was sacred, a home for eternity. Who was any of us to violate that? If we did, we weren't any better than the robbers who forced the builders to play all these elaborate tricks to keep the tomb hidden.

I put the trowel down. Anybody could see what I'd done now, and what shape I'd uncovered. The light caught it just right.

I could cover it up again. But I didn't make any move to do that.

It was almost noon. The air around me was suddenly cold.

I shivered. I could almost see the princess standing in the tunnel, staring at me. Or was it Meritre?

*Now* I was spooked. I got up and turned. I won't say I ran, but I walked awfully fast back up into the light.

# Meru

# Chapter 16

It was a long while and many questions before Lyra could accept that Meru knew nothing about the blue bead or the carefully preserved flower. Finally she let Meru go.

She let her take the bead in its packet with her. Maybe the Decider was hoping that once Meru thought she was by herself, she would stop lying and use the bead for whatever Jian had meant her to use it for.

Meru had not been lying. She could not begin to understand what she was supposed to do. All she could think of was that Jian was not there to ask, and would never be there again.

It did not get easier with time. The dark inside her was deeper, the emptiness more profound, than it had been an hour ago, or a day.

Meru's new cell was high up the levels of Containment, equipped with every luxury but access to the web. It had a clear view of the spaceport and the stilled and silenced cable.

It might have been meant to comfort her. She would not have liked to think that the Decider intended to be cruel.

Meru could eat or drink anything she asked for here. One wall was installed with games and entertainments: primitive, awkward, but better than nothing. She set it to spin through random alternations of music and light, darkened the rest of the walls, and ordered the floor to become a bed.

She curled up with the bead closed tight in her hand. It was thousands of years old, Lyra had said, and it came from Earth. That was another mystery: how Jian had found it and why, and what it had to do with the epidemic in the old city.

Holding the bead that Jian had held, Meru tried to think as Jian might have thought. It helped a little. It brought her mother closer, and blunted the edges of grief.

Consensus had found nothing in or on the bead. It was no more or less than a blue stone bead with a hole drilled through it, wrapped in a package with a flower many thousands of years old. The pictures on the bead's flat bottom were writing, a prayer or incantation in a common and ancient form.

There were thousands of such beads in the world still, stored in museums and temples and old tombs. This one was in no way different, except for the flower that came with it—and there was nothing terribly rare or dangerous about that, either.

Meru needed the web. If Jian had left an explanation anywhere, she would have left it there.

Meru had come close to begging Lyra to restore her access, but something stopped her every time she opened her mouth to try. If Jian had meant Consensus to know what she had found, she would have left the key for them, and not for Meru.

The link was still there, far down in Meru's awareness, with Yoshi on the other end. But it was too weak, the data capacity too small. It could not do much more than make her feel as if she was not alone in the universe.

There was a way to change that.

First, Meru needed to rest. Then she had to find a way out of Containment.

It was a clear plan. It kept her from spinning in the room, screaming with rage and grief and sheer helplessness.

The starwing drifted down from the top of the vault, melted through the cell's walls and surrounded Meru like a blanket. In the wash of its calm and the soothing sound of its purring, she slid into sleep.

She dreamed of that other world, those stiff square walls and unyielding floors. This time the walls were painted from floor to ceiling with strange and brightly colored images, some easy to recognize—an arm and a hand, a bird, a flower—and some not. They were same writing she had seen on the bead.

Everything seemed doubled, as if she was dreaming two dreams at once, but one version was sharper and brighter and seemed newer than the other.

In both, the blue bead rested in a persona's hand: the rounder, paler one that Meru remembered from the odd game on the web, and one almost as narrow but not nearly as dark as Meru's.

The bead was the key. It held the answer to all her questions: the epidemic, the strange game or dream or whatever it was, and the bead itself.

Meru woke to find the starwing gone. It had retreated once more to the roof, feeding on the sunlight that poured through the field.

For a moment she did not remember where she was or why she was there. For the fraction of a second, her world was whole.

Then memory crashed down on her. It flattened her to the floor. She pushed herself up and out of it, and fixed on the thing she had decided to do.

She washed and ate and drank, taking care to be casual. In the cells below, she heard people moving back and forth. Maybe she was imagining that they seemed more agitated than they had when she went to sleep.

That agitation was focused well away from her. She slid a careful glance at the starwing.

It had been waiting for her. It came down and wrapped around her. More than warmth now, she felt a tingle of energy. It was a pleasant sensation, but her skin tightened in case it turned to pain.

The starwing urged her to walk, not too fast, not too slow. An image came to her of a wave rolling toward the shore below the family's house. She matched that speed exactly, as far as she remembered it, and the starwing purred.

She walked out of the cell with no more sensation than a heightening of the tingle and a slight drag at her feet. Once she had passed the field, the starwing grew denser around her, wrapping her in shadow as she walked downward through the levels.

People *were* agitated. They were running, even raising their voices. Invisible in her cloak of alien wings, Meru caught snatches of the conversation.

The plague was spreading. The old city was fully contained, but this morning a child from one of the families had fallen ill.

It was not one of Meru's cousins. She stopped long enough to make sure of that, though the starwing stung her with urgency, nearly betraying them both into visibility.

People were arguing in the central hall, shouting at each other.

"Containment doesn't work! This thing mutates too fast for anything to stop."

"Containment is not the problem. We waited too long to set up the fields. Someone carried it out while we were still ignoring the reports."

"We know it's from offworld—it's been cropping up everywhere out there. We should have looked at the port first, and not diverted all our resources here."

"The first deaths were here. There's been nothing in the port. It's all in the old city or out in the sector. The port is clean. Somehow it skipped straight from the starways to the heart of Earth."

"Does it matter how it got here? This thing got through all our defenses, and now it's spreading. It mutates at an impossible rate; every treatment we find is outdated by the time we finish running the data. Meanwhile, people die."

"Not all of them. Surely—"

"All of them. Once symptoms appear, death occurs within the day. Nothing so far has had the least effect against it."

"Now it's out among the families. We'll have to lock the whole sector down. No one moves anywhere until we find a way to stop this."

"We need the source code—the original form, from which the others have mutated. If we have that, and can track the earliest variations from it, we might be able to predict how it will change. Then we can get ahead of it, anticipate it. We can stop it."

"You haven't found it yet? The first casualties—"

"It had already mutated when the first victim died, and it's kept on mutating. We can't predict what it will do or where it will manifest. There has to have been a carrier, someone who brought it in from offworld."

"The archaeologist? Where was she digging, and what route did she take to Earth?"

"There's nothing there. The planet is clean and so is the ship she traveled in. She avoided the infected worlds on her way here, never touched them at all. She can't have been the carrier. She must have contracted it in the port, or more likely in the old city."

"Then who brought it in? Is it a true carrier—someone who never fell ill, but infected everyone within reach?"

"We don't know."

"We have to know. People are dying!"

Meru dared not stop. She was directly in front of the hall's entrance. A dozen fields overlapped here, taxing the starwing's capacity to stay invisible.

The person who had been talking about Jian was Vekaa. He looked exhausted: his eyes were hollow and his cheeks were sunken. He looked terribly and almost unbearably like his sister after the plague had taken her.

No one here was sick. Meru would have expected someone to mention that, but no one did. Maybe they had argued it to a standstill already.

A man strode out of the hall with a fistful of data beads. He stared directly into Meru's face. She froze.

The starwing hissed. The man turned with no sign of having seen anything and disappeared into one of the cells behind Meru.

She lurched back into motion. For a few precious moments, the way to the outside was clear. People were all in cells or in the center of the sphere, trying to save the world.

The interlocking fields tugged at the starwing. It drew on their energy, darkening around Meru until she could hardly see. All she could think of to do was aim straight ahead.

She dived for the door, squeezed her eyes shut and tumbled through it.

The field burned. The starwing keened in her ear, but it held on. One long, wrenching moment, and then the field was gone.

She stood in the street, wrapped in the starwing. Guards were everywhere, standing in doorways, pacing the street, keeping watch on rooftops.

Out here, there were no warring force fields. Meru kept to the shadows as the persona had in the game when it set out to steal the blue bead.

The persona had called it a scarab. That was a kind of beetle, and also a kind of amulet. Meru slipped her hand into the pocket in which she had been keeping it, and closed her fingers around it.

Fear rose so high she almost lost her will to go on. She was insane to be out here alone, following a rogue data stream and a cryptic scribble. She should go back, slip into the cell again, and let the Deciders find the cure for the plague.

They were doing the best they knew how to do. Meru had Jian's trust and her last message, and a growing conviction that the answer was inside her somewhere. The web, she hoped with all her heart, would be able to tell her where.

As long as there were force fields to feed on, the starwing could keep on hiding her. Her captors had helped it without meaning to, by cutting her off from the web. She was completely invisible. Nothing could track her.

The old city in daylight was if anything more disturbing than it was in the dark. The streets were deserted, and there was no sign of life in the shuttered windows. Door after door was sealed with a symbol Meru had never seen before: a barbed wheel, black on blood red.

Her stomach tightened. What if there were bodies? But she saw nothing that was alive or ever had been, only brick and stone and steel and plascrete.

She had been walking quickly when she left Containment, but by the time she reached the force field that walled off the sector, she was running. The hiss of her own breath, the pounding of her heart, the ache in her legs and lungs, proved with every stride that she was alive, and that she was doing something.

This field hurt much worse than the one around Containment. The scream she heard might have been the starwing's, or it might have been her own. She tripped and fell, tumbling down a flight of steps into a deserted plaza.

She lay winded, struggling to breathe. Her whole body hurt. Her knee was cut; it bled.

After a long while she pulled herself painfully to her feet. The starwing was still wrapped around her, and she hoped it was still protecting her. Its wings had a tattered look, rather like Meru's knee.

It still knew where she had to go. She limped in that direction. As she moved, the pain in her knee eased and the cut began to heal. Even without the web, she still had that protection, part of the implants that had been put in her when she was born.

Guards were moving behind the field. Meru must have triggered an alarm. She limped as fast as she could, ducking into doorways and seeking out shadows.

This sector was as empty as the other. The crowds that she had fought through, the music and laughter she remembered, were gone. Everywhere she went, she was alone; no creature, human or alien, came out to stare at her.

They could not all be dead. They must be hiding, or in Containment.

Meru could not think of so many people gone so quickly, not if she was to go on. She made herself focus on the rest of her escape. There was still the outer field to cross, but the starwing's knowledge base, wherever it came from, showed her a different way than the one that had brought her here. It led her down a flight of steps, this time toward not a blank wall but a broken door.

There was a tunnel behind it. She must have walked down another part of that from the road to the port: it had the same dim and dusty look, and the same fitful procession of lights. It was equally deserted.

Here the starwing could unfold and settle around her neck and rest. The way was mostly straight; if other tunnels merged with it, she chose the widest and brightest.

Her knee was healed. Hunger gnawed at her—healing was hard on the system—but she had nothing to eat or drink.

She could remedy that in the port if she ever got there. She walked as fast as she dared, and trotted or ran when the light was bright enough. She refused to believe that she might be lost. The tunnels had to end eventually. Then, according to the starwing, her way to the port would be clear.

And then—

She would deal with that when she came to it.

# Meru

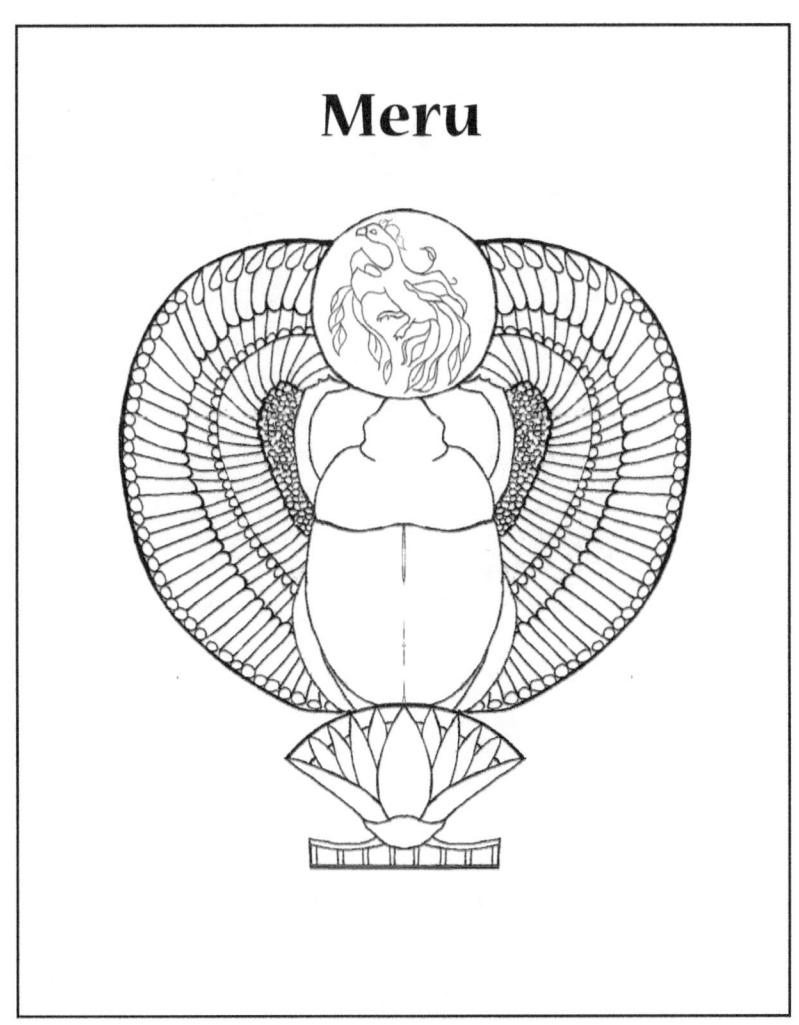

# Chapter 17

**M**eru climbed out of the tunnels into a place so familiar it seemed alien. The cable reared up overhead. Ribbons of roads unrolled around her, connecting the low domes and soaring arches of the port.

She had escaped the old city and its force field altogether. When she touched the web without thinking, to key a search and a map, it was like a dam breaking; a flood of data poured into her head. She stumbled and nearly fell.

Almost too late, she threw up the full firewall, masking her presence and her identity. She had escaped Containment. She did not want to think about the penalty for that.

Even walled off by multiple layers of protection, she was more completely herself than she had been since she went into Containment. A map of the port appeared when she needed it, sparking with links and bits of information. She almost cried, it was so beautiful.

The port was sealed, but the city that surrounded it was as alive as the old city was dead. It was full of people, crowded with travelers who could go nowhere until the ban was lifted.

The whole planet was still on lockdown. She could not take a room without being tagged. She could not buy food or drink, either, or use one of the roads.

Despair dragged at her. She pushed it away. She could do this. Her mother had trusted her.

She needed a place to hide and something to eat, and water to drink.

"Meru."

The link was still there, but strong now, with the full power of the web behind it.

"Yoshi," she said. The rush of gladness died as soon as it was born. "I'm out. I'm free. But you have to forget I exist."

"I don't think so," he said.

Of course he would say that. She should never have said anything. She reached to break the link, to end the connection.

It refused. *He* refused.

"Stupid," she said. "I've broken Consensus. If you get caught—if they find out you have anything to do with me—"

"Too late for that."

That was a real voice. A living person, standing in a doorway past the end of the tunnel.

He was not as tall as she was, and considerably wider: short and stocky and solid. He had a truly formidable scowl.

She scowled back. "Are you insane?"

"Probably." He stepped back through the door.

Meru knew this place. It was a tearoom. She had come here more than once with her mother.

The memory made her throat ache, but it stiffened her spine. She did this for Jian. Nothing could bring her back, but if Meru found the answer to the plague, it would make Jian's death count for something.

Meru and Yoshi wove themselves in among the customers of the café. They attracted no notice. No one was looking for an escaped criminal here.

Consensus itself was protecting her. They could not send out an alarm without starting a panic. There were searchbots everywhere on the web, and searchcams in the city, too, but Meru could elude those.

A server approached. This was a very fine tearoom: the server was human, and physically present.

"Tea," Yoshi said before she could stop him, "and do you have cake?"

"We always have cake," the server said. "Sweet or savory?"

"Both," he said, "and a privacy shield, please."

The server did not even blink. "If privacy is desired, we have a garden of seclusion, which is completely shielded. I'll bring your order there."

Meru lashed at Yoshi through the weblink that they still shared. *Why did you do that? Are you trying to get us caught?*

"I'm hungry," he said in a normal voice. "So are you. We both need to rest and plan."

"The only plan we need is for you to go back home and for me to go on with what I was doing."

"I don't think so," Yoshi said.

Oh, he was stubborn. He was already half a dozen steps ahead of her.

She could just let him go. But then what would she do? She was thirsty and hungry and terribly tired.

She would eat. She would find a way to convince him that if he insisted on helping her, he would probably ruin his life. And then she would do what she had to do.

The garden behind the tearoom was a bubble full of alien plants, strange flowers and stranger creatures that buzzed and flitted and sang. Except for Meru and Yoshi, there was no one in it.

Water bubbled up in a fountain there, and fruit grew on the trees that a human could eat. Meru sat on something like grass under one such tree and breathed in the humid warmth. The starwing flowed through the bubble's field and draped itself over the branches, tossing down fruit for her to catch.

Yoshi stared at it. "Is that what I think it is?"

"It's a starwing," she said.

"You never told us you had one." He was actually hurt. A little angry, even.

"I'm sorry," she said. "Would you have believed me if I had?"

"Yes," he said. Then: "Well. I'd have wanted to see. Because they're so rare. And they can't be tamed."

"They can't," Meru agreed.

He reached, shaking a little, and brushed the edge of a trailing wing.

Meru held her breath. He did not yelp or leap back, and the starwing did not vanish from the bubble. They stared at one another as if fascinated.

The starwing tossed a fruit at his head. He caught it, bit into it, and sat on the grass beside Meru.

His temper had improved tremendously. The tea and cakes arrived while Meru was still pondering what to say, floating in on their own table. There was no sign of the server, and no intrusion on the web.

Yoshi dived for the nearest cake. Meru was a nanosecond behind him.

Yoshi was as ravenous as she was. But Meru's mind kept spinning while she devoured tea and cake and fruit. When she closed her eyes, data streams chased each other across the lids.

"I know what you're thinking," Yoshi said. He finished chewing the next-to-last red bean bun while she reached for the last one. "If we're going to find out where this plague comes from, we have to get into Consensus."

"There's no 'we,'" she said. "You'll never be a starpilot if you get caught helping me."

"If we don't stop this plague, I won't be alive to care."

"Yoshi—"

"Meru. You can't do this alone. Or," he added, "even with a starwing. I've hacked systems before. I scored almost as high as you on that part of the starpilot's examination. I can work my way into a network without being detected."

"A house network," she said. "Or school. And they weren't hunting for you. For this, I have to hack the world."

"That's why you need me. Someone has to back you up. What if you get caught? Or maybe worse—trapped in the system?"

She shuddered. She had been trying not to think about that.

She tried one last time to save him from himself. "Go now. Just leave."

He folded his arms and set his face and made it clear he was going nowhere.

She glanced at the starwing. It ignored her. As far as she could tell anything of how it felt, it liked Yoshi. It wanted him to stay.

"Traitor," she said to it.

"It knows what you need," Yoshi said. "You start. I'll follow."

There really was no choice. Not if she wanted to get this done before Consensus found her.

She slipped the scarab from its pocket and cradled it in her palm, rubbing the incised bottom lightly with her thumb. Yoshi's curiosity brushed past her on the web, but he asked no questions. He was simply there, waiting, ready to move wherever she needed him to go.

She was already slipping away into that deepest of all deep portions of the web. She felt again the multiplying of sensation: her hand, the pale round hand, the thin brown one. They fit one on top of the other, all holding the scarab.

That was important. It meant something. She had to know what it was: a need so strong it knotted her stomach.

She plugged keywords into the web. *Scarab. Key. Plague. Triple.*

Data streams flooded her interfaces. The scarab *was* the key—to the web, to the epidemic, and to something completely different. Something that had to do with the three hands that had held this same blue bead.

*Triple.* She followed a single stream among the countless trillions, one definition of a simple and common word, that led to a most uncommon concept—suggestion—theory.

She looked into a mirror that reflected not her own dark, narrow, big-eyed face but a long pale-brown oval, green-eyed, with hair neither straight nor curly and neither gold nor brown. That one looked through another mirror at a softer oval, red brown, with long dark eyes heavily painted, and perfectly straight, thick and shining, blue-black hair.

The data streams marked and dated them. Pre-Stellar, Pre-Collapse, dawn of the web: that was the green-eyed one. The other, the one beyond her, was at least as old again: Egypt in the days of its empire, before there was even a dream of the web.

If what the data stream hinted at was true, the other two were not constructs on the web or personas in a game. They were alive. They had lived. They were real.

"Of course I'm real," said the one in the middle. "You're the imaginary one. You don't even exist yet."

"I do too exist," Meru said. "It seems we all exist. And this"—she brushed the scarab with a virtual finger—"is the thing that binds us."

"I don't think," said the most ancient of them, "that an amulet alone completes the spell. It's larger than that. Stronger."

"But it lets us see each other," the one in the middle said. She narrowed her eyes at Meru. "Meredith. My name is Meredith."

"Meredith," Meru said. It was a sort of apology.

"And Meritre," said the oldest of them all, though in her own world she was as young as the rest. "It's good we give each other the gift of names. Names matter."

"Maybe they're a part of it, too," Meredith said. "It's like time travel. But—bigger. Somehow."

"Yes," Meru said. "Yes." She hung on the edge of something enormous—some knowledge that would change the world.

The pieces of it clicked together, one, two, three. Three pairs of eyes met across the millennia.

"I think I get what you're doing," Meredith said. "You're web searching, right? We have the web, too. Much smaller. Much, much more simple. We can't link directly to it. Yet. But soon. I think. We're close."

"You are," Meru allowed. "Yes, I am searching."

"I don't know what this web is," said Meritre, "though it seems to have something to do with what spiders do—threads woven into a pattern, yes? Like certain kinds of magic. Magic of weaving, and of patterns. But also magic of words. Words are power. Speak them just so, and they can break worlds."

"Or make them," Meru said.

"Those are best of all," said Meritre.

Carefully she closed her fingers over Meredith's, and over Meru's. "Let us be hunters of words. Where do we begin?"

Now there was a question. "Stay with me," Meru said. "See what I do. If something looks familiar, tell me."

"I can do that," Meritre said. Meredith, between them, nodded.

Her face was tight. Meru's felt much the same.

That was comforting, in a strange way. She used that fear to sharpen her senses; to deepen and broaden the search.

As little good as it did. Every search string led to the same blank wall. *Access Forbidden.*

The first, she bounced off, startled. The second, she tried a sub-string, and for an instant was sure she had breached the wall. Just as she braced herself to slip through the crack, it slammed shut.

The third wall rose up like a storm of fire. It seared her edges; it licked toward her center. She reeled backward.

The Egyptian reached through her. It was clumsy, because she could not have ever done such a thing before, but she found her balance remarkably quickly.

"Keywords," she said. "Search strings. Here we call them incantations. They fit into patterns. Look; see."

"I can't—" Meru stopped. Yes, she could see. The search strings clicked together in particular and perceptible ways—ways that led to a trap.

"Something doesn't want us nosing around in here," Meredith said. She sounded a little breathless, as if she was fending off fear.

"My mother died for those answers," Meru said, very level and very calm.

Neither of those things had anything to do with how she felt inside. She reeled herself in before she did something frustrated and angry and very badly advised.

Meritre was not paying attention. She was singing to the web and the wall. "Ra of the Horizon, Ra-Harakhte, Mother Isis, Great Osiris, hear us. Look on us. Guide us. Grant us the key to the door; the secrets of the plague; the truth of those who live in threes, who dwell in the house of life, from age to age and into eternity."

She had a beautiful voice. Its clarity pierced through the hiss of the fire. The words it carried took shape in the web, shaping patterns that Meru could not have imagined, search strings bound to concepts that no one in her world would have thought of.

The trap dissipated in a cloud of random data. They all slid through, the three of them bound together into a single persona.

"Whoa," said Meredith, just as Meru said, "What did you—"

"I gave it my heart," Meritre said.

Someday Meru would understand that. Maybe. For now it was enough that it had worked.

Though what it had worked on, she was not exactly sure. There was nothing there except another reference, a pointer to a database that had long since been taken out of Earth's web. Meru would have howled, if it would not have brought the whole web down on her.

"What's the matter?" Meredith's voice was sharp. "What is this? Why aren't you celebrating?"

"Because it's not an answer!" Meru almost shouted back. "It's barely even a question. And it's not here. Not on Earth's web. It's out *there*."

She flung her hand outward, toward the near-infinite ocean of the interstellar web. "Starpilots go to school for years to learn how to surf that web. I haven't even set foot off Earth yet. I'm good. I'm well trained—for Earth. But this..."

"We have to try," Meredith said. "We're here, aren't we? That must mean something. We've got a key, somehow. Somewhere in us is a password to the locked data."

"Maybe it's the scarab," Meritre said. "Have you read what it says? It's a simple prayer, but then there is nothing simple about prayer."

"Why not?" Meredith said. "It couldn't hurt."

With no expectation of anything happening, but because she could not think if anything else to do, Meru gave the web the inscription on the scarab's bottom, exactly as it was carved, in writing that almost no one alive could read.

The firewall fell. All the data in the universe roared and surged around her. Warnings flashed and strobed and screamed.

*Forbidden! Felony! Unauthorized entry! Insufficient clearance! Do not enter! Do not enter! Do not enter!*

The storm of data reduced Meru to an infinitesimally tiny speck. Before she could quite wink out, the starwing's insubstantial warmth wrapped around her. At the same time she felt a hand in each of hers: one shorter and wider, and one wiry and narrow.

The Triple was still together. Still holding on.

"You have us," Meredith said. "You are real."

"*We* are real," said Meritre. "We are whole."

The starwing trilled and spread its wings. It was as much at home riding the streams of data as it was soaring on the physical winds of Earth.

And why not? The web was energy, and so was the starwing, mostly. Who knew; maybe this was its native environment.

All three humans rode inside the creature like passengers in a starship. The data stream that had brought them there glimmered ahead of them. Meru sent the starwing after it, skimming the streams and darting through eddies and currents.

At the edge of a wave of data, just before the stream melted into it, Meritre caught it. Meredith batted it back toward Meru. Meru triggered *Save*, and then, *Download*.

Even as she captured the last of it, the web turned against her. Security bots swarmed over her. The starwing melted from around her. She hardly had time to react to the betrayal before she crashed out of the web.

# Meru

# Chapter 18

I'm sorry," Yoshi said. He did not look apologetic. He looked furious.

The Guards had emptied the café and sealed it, turning it into its own Containment unit. Two of them held Yoshi. They were much bigger than he was, but they looked remarkably ruffled. One had a bruise on her cheek.

"I tried to keep them out," he said. "But my hack got hacked. It didn't hold."

"You are good," Vekaa said. "If you make it as far as your own starship, you'll do well."

"I fully intend to," Yoshi said.

Meru was dizzy and dazed from her deep search and the things she had found there. The two strangest were still inside her, watching in silence, living these hours with her.

She drew a deep breath. Her uncle and her friend started as if she had let out a shout.

*Where* were *you?* Yoshi demanded through their link that had not broken in spite of everything. *You just suddenly evaporated. I could see you sitting there. You were breathing, your eyes were open, but you were gone. Totally vanished from the web. I couldn't find you anywhere.*

*I went deep,* she said. *And then out. Off Earth. Then I got cut off.*

It was not all of the story, not by half. She could tell he knew it. *Later,* he said. *Tell me.*

She could not have answered even if she had wanted to. Vekaa had her by the shoulders, shaking her.

He caught himself. He looked as startled as she felt. Cool, contained Vekaa never cracked. Never let go.

He drew himself up and composed himself with visible effort. "I'm not even going to ask what you were thinking," he said. "Did it never occur to you that we might have let you go?"

"It might have," she said. "I didn't find anything. Have you?"

He closed his eyes, then opened them. "No. Nothing new. Except new mutations of the disease."

"Nothing offworld?"

"Nothing yet," he said.

"Maybe," Meru said slowly, as the thought took shape, "it's not alien. Maybe it's one of ours."

"That can't be," he said. "We've isolated or eradicated every virus and bacillus that can affect the human body. The only diseases that can touch us now come from the stars—and we've armored ourselves against them."

"I can see that," Meru said. "It's in the all the data streams, right off the official feed. But I can see something else, too. Even with no mention of *plague* or *epidemic,* people know what the word you are using means. It's a *situation.* You're telling them to stay home. Not travel. Wait for further instructions. Don't you think that's making them afraid?"

"They're braver than you may think," Vekaa said, "and we are working hard to find the cause. We will find it. Soon."

"With respect," Yoshi said, and his tone was indeed respectful, "if we can hack the system, so can others. The news is going to break. What if you haven't found the answer yet? What then?"

"Then the Deciders will decide what to do," said Vekaa.

"And we are keeping you from your work."

Vekaa shook his head slightly, but he did not deny it. "We who work in Containment are at wits' end. The organisms we study have all been thoroughly tamed. All the wild ones that survived have stayed safely offworld. And yet this is one is wild beyond capture. And it is here."

Meru had never heard him speak so bluntly before. He had been closer to Jian than anyone but Meru. His world breaking. And so, she could see, was he.

"Uncle," she said, and she tried to be gentle, "may we go home? We'll promise not to run again. As long as we're all on lockdown, can't we be locked down with our families? I think—I need—"

She was not feigning the catch of tears in her voice. If she was using it to get what she needed, she told herself, it was for a good cause. She would help them if she could. She would save them all—if it was possible.

"That is fair enough," said Lyra's voice. Her face materialized in the air, drawn off the web. "She takes up resources that we need to fight this thing. Send her home and order your family to keep her under surveillance pending judgment, and come back to your laboratory. Make sure she really is locked down."

The Decider's face winked out. Vekaa bowed his head to the shimmer where it had been.

When he turned to Meru, she could see how torn he was between duty and grief. He covered it quickly with the same cold stillness that had been in Lyra's face and voice. "Should we trust you?"

That was fair, though it stung. She answered him as coolly as she could. "I can keep searching the web from home, if you don't cut me off again. That's all I wanted to do."

"It wasn't my decision," he said. She heard the pain there, quickly and firmly suppressed. "You realize you haven't been judged yet. There will be a penalty."

Meru swallowed. She was afraid she knew what it would be. But she could not have done it differently.

One thing she still had to say. "Whatever you do to me, let Yoshi go. I'll take all the responsibility—and all the penalty. Don't punish him for what I've done."

"No," said Yoshi. "No, you don't. I'm part of this. I'm not leaving till it's done. And I'm not letting you do all the paying. We're both responsible. If we go down, we go together."

Meru did not look at him. She kept her eyes on Vekaa. "He is a good friend," she said. "Please let him go home, and be safe, and be free."

"He can be safe," Vekaa said, "but he can't go home. The whole continent is on lockdown. All the roads and the airways and the tunnels under the seas are closed. I'll send him home with you." He turned to Yoshi. "You will be welcome in the house of Banh-Liu."

Yoshi bowed politely. "I will be honored," he said.

He was very kindly refraining from gloating where Meru could see. She could hardly object: he was her friend; she wanted him to be safe.

Completely safe. Not bound up in this thing that she was bound in, for which she would very likely lose her dream of the stars. She did not want him to lose the stars.

Vekaa took her hand. His fingers were warm and his clasp was firm. "Come," he said, "and promise me. If you find anything, tell me."

"I will if I can," she said.

That was slippery phrasing, but he let it go. She was free to go home, and nowhere else. The bubble he sealed her into with Yoshi was set for the family's entrance code, and would not stop or unlock before it reached the house on the headland.

Yoshi stretched out on the floor of the bubble as it began to move down the road. For the first time she could see how tired he was.

"Go to sleep," she said. "I'll wake you before we get home."

He eyed her warily. "You're still mad at me."

"Not really," she said. "Just annoyed. And afraid for you."

"I can take care of myself," he said. Even while he said it, he yawned.

"Sleep," she said.

He could hardly help it. His eyes drooped; he drew a deep breath. His whole body let go at once, falling into sleep.

She was exhausted; she had been awake for days. But there was no sleep in her. She would rest when this was over.

The sun was setting over the port and the sea. With her new and intermittent threefold vision, she also saw it hanging low over a landscape of wide brown river and stark red cliffs and pitiless blue sky.

The other two were in the same place, though separated by thousands of years. It was not the same place Meru was in. What she could gather from Meredith, who knew what the whole planet was shaped like, pointed to a location well south and east of the starport.

With their curiosity and barely controlled eagerness to urge her on, she opened the data stream she had pulled off the greater web. It was a small thing, a spurt of information. First, a timeline, marked off in equal thirds. Then, a human figure standing at the point of each third.

It was the same figure in all three, though it wore a different costume in each. The note attached to it said, *Some in this world live in threes. Three eras, three lives, one self. See 'Triple,' 'Triad,' 'Transmigration of Souls.'*

None of those keywords led to an active link, though Earth's web offered a flood of irrelevant data. All she gained from that was an overview of ancient religion, magic, and superstition.

"That makes no sense," Meru said.

"But it does," said Meredith. "I know it shouldn't. I've never heard of anything like it." Through the link they shared, Meru felt how she wavered between incredulity and a kind of stunned belief.

Meru shared the incredulity. The rest… "It's not possible," she said.

"Except it is," Meredith said. "Because here we are. What I don't understand—what I don't quite get—"

"I…think I do," Meritre said. "We're the same person. All our souls are one—one being. We've lived each of these lives, and who knows how many others, but we can talk to each other. We can know what we were and what we'll be."

"Yes," Meredith said. "And because we know all that, we can change the flow of time."

"Time is a river," Meritre said. "I'm here, down in Waset, and you're in the middle, and she—she's almost to the sea."

"Right," said Meredith. Her voice shook a little.

Meru was shaking all over. Part of it was anger at herself. How could these ancients, these creatures of times so old they could barely comprehend this world she lived in, be so much quicker to understand what was happening?

"Now that is just rude," Meredith said. "Maybe you're so advanced you've forgotten how to see the obvious."

Meru sucked in a breath. Before she could burst out, Meritre said, "That doesn't help anything. We are here, and we are real, and so the rest must be real, too. There must be something we are destined to do. Or why do we exist at all?"

"Simply because we exist," Meredith said. Then she added quickly, "No, no, that's rude, too. It's all so…it's crazy. Wild. Unimaginable. But it *is*."

Meru hated to agree, but she had no other or better answer. "Even our names are alike," she said. "Which is maybe a coincidence, and maybe not."

"Yes," said Meritre. "It's a great magic."

"It makes my head hurt," Meredith said.

Meru's head was aching, too. Her world had been full of wonders and strangeness, but it had been safe, because she thought she understood it. Now she understood that it was stranger than she had ever imagined—stranger and more deadly.

But more wonderful, too. There were three of her. All so different, all so strange to one another. But all the way down at the root, they were the same.

The bubble left the mainland and sped over the sea. Meru could see the family's house now, a cluster of walls and domes that seemed to grow out of the cliff. Others rose up in towers or grew like crystals, scattered across the island.

The strangers inside Meru shared visions of their own cities. Meredith showed her a complex mixture of glass and stone and steel, tall towers and low squat houses and everything between. Through Meritre's eyes she saw a city of enormous stone halls and lower, darker mud-brick structures that used to be full of people, but less so now, since the plague.

Meru went very, very still. "Plague?"

The word struck her with the force of memory, but it was nothing she had known in this life. She heard the coughing, smelled the stink of blood and death, and saw the bodies piled in boats, waiting to be ferried across to the desert.

It was not the same disease that she had seen in the old city. No one had been coughing there. Their lungs filled first, and their organs melted inside the skin.

Still, it was a connection, which was better than anything Consensus had. Maybe it would lead to an answer.

# Meredith

# Chapter 19

It had happened. We'd broken through. It took Meru with her interstellar web, and the scarab for all of us to focus on, but we'd done it; we were aware of each other. We could communicate.

The reason for that was still too much for me to get my mind around. I wasn't ready to face not just reincarnation but—this. Whatever it was.

My first impulse, as usual, was to reach for my phone. But who could I call? Who would believe it? I could barely manage that myself, and I was living it.

"Magical objects do concentrate the mind," Meritre said inside my head, heart, wherever she was—Meru's web made as much sense as anything else. "And words can connect a mind to the actual thing."

You'd think, as far back as she was, with technology that hadn't even got to the wheel yet, that she'd be the most confused, but she understood all this at least as well as the rest of us. If I was going to be honest, she understood it best of all.

"I set out to work a spell to save my family," she said. "I'm still going to do that, if I possibly can. But this goes much further. What I thought I was seeing, what I wanted to do, was too small. My eyes looked too low. Now I've lifted them, and I can see across thousands of years."

She thought in patterns—in stories. I did, too. I had a few thousand more years of them to draw on, and when I looked at them, really looked, I saw something that might be a complete coincidence. Or it might be the answer Meru was looking for.

"Look," I said. "Meru, your mother left a clue: the scarab we've all got, and flower that's as old, maybe, as Meritre. Something preserved that flower for an impossibly long time."

Meritre's eyes lit up with understanding, all the way down the river of time. "A tomb," she said. "Where we preserve the dead for everlasting, with all that they wanted or needed in life, and as many of their belongings as they could wish to have with them. And flowers, for the sweetness, and for remembrance."

"My mother is—was—always digging in tombs," Meru said. I heard the catch of her voice when she changed from present to past. I felt the rush of grief, so strong it choked me.

It nearly threw me out of whatever this was. I'd just heard that my mom was going to be dead, if she wasn't already. Meru knew for a fact that her mother was dead.

I had to wrench my mind away from that and focus on the questions we needed to ask, if we were going to get answers. Maybe it was all imaginary and I was going completely crazy. I didn't care. It was something to think about besides the unthinkable.

"We have a plague here," Meritre said. "It's nearly past. The gods have taken their final sacrifice. Our princess is with the embalmers. When their work is done, she'll go into her tomb."

"The tomb we're looking for," I said. "The one somewhere around the mortuary temple. Do you think—"

Meru went on for me. "Can that be where it came from? That ancient plague survived somehow, and found its way to the stars, then spread so far and so long that no one even remembers where it started? But it started on Earth—and my mother found it. She tracked it to its source."

"Earth," I said. "Egypt. But how could a virus survive for thousands of years?"

Meritre heard *virus* as *demon*, which made sense to her. "Demons might scatter to the winds, but they never really die. Some part of them can last forever. Maybe if people can find them and get control of them, they can be forced to work spells that cure the plague."

What's a virus, when you think about it, but a really small and really dangerous demon? And what's a vaccine but a kind of spell that uses the demon's own power to destroy it?

Meru saw it, too. She nodded, away on the far end of time. "It must have been in the tomb the flower came from."

"The scarab wasn't in the tomb," I said. "They found it in a tunnel that they thought didn't lead anywhere. Except—"

I stopped. I'd found a door. What if—

"Meritre," I said. "Do you know where the tomb is?"

"Oh, no," she said. "That's always a secret. Nobody knows, except the few who work in it."

Of course she wouldn't know. That would be too easy. It would all fit together so nicely then. Meru would have her answer, and she could give it to her uncle, and her world would be safe.

Neat. Tidy. Nothing like the world I found myself in.

I couldn't stand it any more. I let them slip away, sliding out of sight down Meritre's river of time.

I hadn't said a word to anyone in my world about the door at the end of the tunnel. I'd probably blow up the universe if I kept quiet, but I didn't care.

I sat in my room in Luxor House with the door locked and the laptop on, clicking through screen after screen of silly and stupid. The sillier and stupider, the better. I answered all my e-mail with chirpy variations on "Hi! I'm having a great time! I've posted on my blog! Go see!"

The blog was all about digging and labeling and what we had for lunch and how Jonathan liked to play Abba songs that his crew sang along with in Arabic, and if you haven't heard "Dancing Queen" sung to a belly-dance beat, you haven't been living the crazy life. I didn't mention Dad or Kelly. I didn't mention Mom. Above all, I didn't mention Meru and Meritre.

While I was noodling uselessly and wasting time because doing anything real was too bloody terrifying, the new-email alert went off. It was from Cat, and it was a picture of Bonnie from a few seconds ago. She was all white and shimmery from a bath, and she was eating—of course. The look in her eye said she knew she was getting her picture taken, and she knew why, and she knew everything I'd been thinking and doing.

Every. Crazy. Thing.

My throat locked up. I missed her so much.

I shut my eyes. I could smell her, and feel her smooth satiny coat under my hand.

She blew on my palm, and nipped it just enough to sting. But when I opened my eyes, there wasn't anything there. Just the picture on the screen, and complete craziness inside my head.

Meru was chasing data across a web that made my Internet look like smudges on a cave wall. Meritre sat on the roof with the cat in her lap, watching the stars come out over the temple. People were talking nearby, speaking ancient Egyptian, but I knew what they were saying.

I knew because I was Meritre. Those voices in the dark, all warm and comfortable with each other, belonged to my people, too. I *knew* them.

The rioting had stopped. The city was calm again. People had picked up and carried on, and some were doing better than they had before.

Meritre had worked her spell with Djehuti's assistance. He'd agreed at the time that it wouldn't hurt anything, and would probably help.

Tonight she was sure of it. Meritre's father was talking to Uncle Amonmose about his wonderful new promotion. "The king herself spoke to me," he said, "and asked me to carve the most important statue I may ever carve: the *ka* statue of the princess, may she live for everlasting."

Uncle Amonmose hissed in awe. "Oh! That is indeed wonderful. But well deserved. You have the best eye among the sculptors, and the best hand, too."

"That's as may be," said Meritre's father. "It was my turn. I'll do my best, and that's as good as it will get."

From Meritre, and from things Aunt Jessie had told me, too, I understood what they were saying. A *ka* statue was a mighty magic, an exact image of the person who had died. It represented the part of her soul that would stay in the tomb.

When he finished it, it would stand in its own special room, with a narrow slit of a door that let it come and go. It could eat the food that another artist painted on the walls, and it could also eat whatever the family left for it.

It was a huge honor. Meritre was so proud she almost cried. She was also glad, because it meant her father could work in a smaller shop, carving in wood, and not breathe the stone dust that made him cough up blood in the evenings.

She sat and stroked the cat into a purring puddle, and listened to the voices going back and forth. Her eyes weren't on either of them. They were on the shadow beside Amonmose that was Djehuti.

She liked Djehuti. A lot.

I could see it. Horse nerds like me are more apt to get squealy over somebody's new horse than somebody's new boyfriend, but dress Djehuti in shorts and a tank and put him on the beach at Vero and he'd have every girl within range fighting over who got to ask him out first.

Meritre wasn't squealy. She was quiet. She liked looking at Djehuti. She liked talking to him.

He liked it, too. He slid away from Amonmose, all casual, as if it didn't matter nearly as much as it did. With one thing and another, by the time he'd finished wandering around the roof and smelling the flowers, I could tell he'd be sitting beside Meritre.

She was my age, but most of her friends were married or about to be, if they were still alive. Life was shorter here; people grew up faster.

It was still life. She was alive and breathing and she wanted to keep on doing it, along with her parents and her friends and even her brothers. She cared about the things I cared about.

This Triple thing didn't seem to bother her. She was used to thinking of everybody as having at least four souls. Why shouldn't one of them live different lives on its way to eternity?

I'd been mocking Meru for not being able to deal. But now I'd had time to think about it. "I can't take it," I said. "I don't want to do this any more."

Meritre stopped petting the cat, which rolled onto its back and wrapped paws around her arm and made her start again. "It's not a game," she said. "It's a gift we've all been given. The gods want something of us in return. My plague has ended; Meru's just beginning. We can help save a world."

"Look," I said, "not that I don't respect your religion, but we don't believe in it any more. There aren't any gods. There's no magic. All we have is what we are."

"Yes," she said, and she didn't even blink. "Look at what we are. Isn't it proof that the gods exist?"

Here I was, sitting with my laptop in my lap instead of the tortie cat that I'd locked out with the rest of the world, arguing about religion with someone who lived four thousand years ago. That was just crazy. But, God— not that I believed in the cranky old guy with the beard and the lightning bolt—it felt real.

I could feel the cat's fur under my fingers. I could smell the smoke from the cooking fires, and hear a hollow booming sound that Meritre knew was a crocodile in the river. Something would die tonight, and the crocodile would have its dinner.

"That's just sick," I said.

She looked through my eyes at a room that made sense to her because it was four walls and a floor, but the laptop didn't mean anything, and I didn't know what she'd make of a Land Rover or a telephone or an airplane.

"The shining bird," she said: "the hawk of Horus. You rode inside it. What a wonder, to be able to fly!"

I felt that wonder. I felt how amazing it all was. So much magic, so much power, and I hardly even noticed it.

My world, to me, was just ordinary. To her, it was the wildest of all wild stories.

She loved this. I hated it. "What difference does it make if we save someone else's world? What if we do cure Ebola or whatever it is her people are getting? It doesn't save anything here. It doesn't cure cancer."

"I am sorry about your mother," she said. I could feel how much she meant it. "Maybe there's a spell that can help her. Maybe the other one, the one who flies through the stars, would know—"

"I'm sure she does," I said, "but the science—the magic spell—would be too advanced. Whatever it takes, we don't have now. We aren't that far along."

"Maybe you are meant to be. Because of what you know."

I would love to believe that. Really and truly I would. But I know what's real and what isn't. "Things like that—magic, whatever—have to grow. They don't just happen. There are steps that lead to them. We aren't anywhere near there yet."

She nodded. It was weird, because I could feel as well as see her doing it. "The great magics are the work of years. You have days."

I wanted to smack her. Cold-hearted little bitch. What did she know about what I was feeling? *Her* mother was alive and well and sitting in the dark with her hands resting over her swelling middle, listening to the men go on about temples and tombs.

That wasn't fair. I knew it wasn't. I didn't care.

I shut it off. I pulled the plug on the whole thing. I dived into the stupidest, crappiest, sparkly-unicorn-iest website I could possibly find, and drowned in pink curly paragraphs and oceans of exclamation points.

The unicorn flapping its wings and batting its eyelashes around the pages made me think of Meru's starwing. How amazing it was. How totally alien. How I just wanted to swat it.

"I quit," I said. "I'm out. Save your own damned world."

# Meru

# Chapter 20

**M**eru lay alone in the dark. For the first time since she could remember, she had blacked out the stars.

Waves of grief for her mother came and went. Down below in the family's house, everyone else was meeting, discussing the news and coming to agreement as to what to do about it.

She should have been there. No one forced her, and no one particularly wanted her there. She was in disgrace and worse. She had committed a crime; she had disgraced the family.

That mattered much less than it might have once. The passion to know and understand, to find an answer that led to a cure for the disease that her mother had tracked to Earth and then died of, was still there. So was the conviction that no matter what happened, she had to get offworld. She had to become a starpilot.

It had all tangled up together when Meredith-in-the-middle shut herself out. Without her, nothing Meru did could reach down eight thousand years to Meritre, who might, who just might, know where to find the answer. She was out of range of whatever it was that made the connection possible.

They both needed the middle in order to find each other. And the middle had disappeared.

The starwing stirred in the dark, trilling to itself. Usually when it moved it was silent, but she heard its wings rustle. It came and curled up against her side.

The lift door whispered open. Yoshi stepped through: a shadow against the dazzle of light from inside.

The light winked out. Yoshi inched cautiously toward her. "Is this where you always go? To lie in the dark?"

"No," she said.

"Ah," said Yoshi.

Suddenly there were stars. Not only the stars of Earth, far out on its galactic arm, but stars upon stars upon stars.

He had found the feed from the center, from the galaxy's heart. The light fell like rain; it blazed, it blinded, it emptied her of everything but itself.

"Better?" Yoshi asked.

"Better," she admitted. "Am I cast out of the family yet?"

"Not that I can tell," he said. "They're arguing about Ulani now. Did you know she wants to join Family Cordere-Marais? She's in love, she says. She wants to live in the sea, she says. She's already applied for the body modifications."

Meru sat up straight. "She has not!"

"She has," Yoshi said.

"But she wouldn't," Meru said. "Not without telling me first. I knew about Aracele Marais, she's been talking about her for—oh, ever. But to move there? To turn into a *fish*?"

"Maybe you weren't there to talk to," he said. "You've been a little preoccupied."

Guilt stabbed, sudden and sharp. That night when Meru left to find her mother—Ulani's pauses and shufflings had meant something. She had been trying to tell Meru about her decision. And Meru had not even noticed.

"I've only been trying to save the world," Meru said to that memory as much as to the boy in front of her.

As soon as she had said it, she realized how nasty it sounded. And arrogant.

She *was* arrogant. She expected everything to be about her. Ulani had changed her life without asking Meru first. And the family had been discussing her all this time down below, instead of Meru.

Meru had done something terrible, and probably criminal. Consensus would demand a price for that. But that was done; there was no changing it.

Ulani was about to do something that would change her life, and the family's life. *She* could change her course, if they all came to consensus. That was at least as important to the family.

Life did not stop because the world was trying to end. Or because Meru was trying to save it.

The starwing pressed closer, as if it could sense the tangle of her emotions.

It was pressing against the pocket with the stasis field in it. She shifted away from that small discomfort, and slipped the flower and the scarab out into her palm.

The scarab was more than a connection to Meru's other lives. Jian had held it, too, and discovered somehow what it was and what it could do, if it came into the right hands.

Maybe Meru did not need Meredith. Maybe she had the knowledge here, in her mother's memories.

"Yoshi," she said. "I'm going back on the web—down deep, where I was before. My mother left a message inside the clue. I have to try to find it."

"I'll go with you," he said.

"I'm not sure you can," she said. "It's—keyed just to me. But if you can watch; make sure I find my way back again—"

"I can do that," he said. "But, Meru—"

"Thank you," she said.

She did not wait for him to start a new argument. She plugged the scarab's inscription back into her search bots, but this time she added Jian's name to the string.

As if it had been waiting for her to do just that, a data stream collided with her search bot and burst open.

The sky was lavender and the sun was dim, more red than yellow. Stars shone at midday.

Jian sat inside a dome above a sea of mercury, looking out across the waves of shimmering, surging silver. Most of the faces and forms in the dome behind her were alien, but the man who sat beside her was a perfectly ordinary human.

Ordinariness was a mask he wore. Jian doubted that the face she saw was the one he had been born with, and she knew that his name was just a designation. He called himself Grey.

There were creatures like him all through the known worlds. They bought and sold knowledge; they traded in rumors and in facts, usually without distinction.

Most of what they had to sell was useless or worse. But once in a great while, and often unexpectedly, they happened on a glimmer of gold.

She looked down at the data bead he had given her. Inside was the image of a blue bead carved in the shape of a beetle, with an inscription in a very old language indeed. The bead's wrapping was equally old: a scrap of paper made from coarse brownish fibers, and a mummified flower.

She almost laughed—at herself; at the hope she had still, after all these years and so many disappointments, dared to believe in. "This is from Earth," she said. "It's a common thing; there are thousands of them scattered across the worlds. What does it have to do with the answers I've been looking for?"

"Perhaps everything," he said. "Perhaps nothing. You are a seeker after answers. This is an answer to one of many questions."

Jian bit back a sharp rejoinder. What she allowed herself to say was not particularly gentle, either, but it was, at least, somewhat restrained. "That, if I may be so blunt, means exactly nothing. I came half across the galaxy on your promise of clear and certain information. Now you give me wind and platitudes." She rose. "Others may have more patience for this game you play. I have no time, or credit, to waste."

"Time is running short," he said, "indeed. For your search. For the proof you have been seeking."

She shook her head, making no further effort to hide her impatience. She turned on her heel, focused already on the exit; reaching out to the web for the schedule of flights away from this world, back to the site she had been excavating. That she should never have left, no matter how urgent the call.

Grey was there on the web, blocking her access. His voice behind her said, "These are the questions you have asked, over and over through all your travels: *What is the cause of all this ruin? What was it that killed these worlds? Where does it come from? Where is it going?*"

She stopped, spun. "More of the obvious."

He smiled. It was not a warm smile, nor a comfortable one. "You have an answer to the last. Do you not? It is moving. Circling. Turning back. Mutating as it goes. Your projections and mine—they agree. They know where it will strike next."

"Earth is protected," she said.

"Is it?"

"Oh, no," she said. "You'll not cripple me with false fear."

"I merely asked a question," he said, "as you do." He tilted his head toward the data bead. "There is an answer here."

"Why? How do you know? Where did you find this?"

"Just as any seeker of knowledge would," said Grey. "I know a person who knows a person who heard a rumor who found a reference to a discovery that might be of interest. I made the connections. I found the sources. The rest is yours to resolve. For," he added delicately, "of course, a suitable consideration."

"Why?"

"Why does any being wish to make a living?"

She bared her teeth. "That is not what I asked. Why is it mine to resolve?"

"Because of who and what you are, and what you have been hunting for; and because of the world from which you come."

"Earth?" she said. "Are you implying that the plague originated there? That theory is old and rather extensively discredited. There is no single planet of origin for the waves of disease that run through the worlds."

"That is true," he said, "but certain strains have begun in one place and spread with the expansion of space travel, and mutated as they traveled."

Jian had learned to trust no one, least of all a being who pandered to her own convictions. She believed that the cultures she studied had all been brought down by the same virus, one that happened to be ravaging a swath of worlds even now. She also believed, and in that she was all but alone, that the original strain had come from Earth.

"Even if what you say were so," she said to this man, or whatever he was, "what can you offer me that I haven't so far discovered for myself?"

"Very little, in truth," he said, "but you would do well to ask yourself yet another question. Your world has eradicated all diseases that can endanger the human organism, or so it believes. Is it absolutely sure of that?"

"After a thousand years, I would think it might be."

"Indeed, you would think," he said.

She paused. Counted breaths. Remembered calm. "Tell me why I should believe you. I've been led into traps before. How am I to know this is not another?"

"I may be no friend to you," he said, "but I'm not your enemy. Find the original of this. The rest, my sources assure me, will come clear."

"Your sources? What are they? Who are they? Where do they come from? What—"

He did not answer that, only smiled that uncomfortable smile.

Jian reached toward him. She did not know if she meant to strike him or shake him or simply push him away.

It hardly mattered. He was gone.

She might have believed that he was a very good simulacrum, if the data bead had not still been in her hand. That was real. The artifact it led to was real as well. So was the country, and the culture, that it had come from.

If Earth was in danger, this could be the best and only warning it would get.

Consensus must know. She was one person; they were billions. If the plague had reached Earth, surely they were taking steps to destroy it.

She should send the data to her brother, along with a recording of her meeting with Grey. Epidemiology was Vekaa's specialty, after all, and she was certain that Grey, or whoever had sent him, knew that. Vekaa would deal with it, and she would go back to the expedition that was waiting for her.

But as she stood by that window above that alien sea, she knew she could do no such thing. If this really was the proof she had been searching for, she had to hunt it down herself. She had to know; she had to be sure.

She had to do it quickly. Her daughter would be leaving Earth very soon, traveling to the orphan planet where the young of a hundred worlds trained to become starpilots. If the virus really had mutated into a form that could infect Earthlings in spite of all their protections, Meru could get sick. She could die.

But that was not the worst of it. If Grey's implication was true, and the mutated virus was already on Earth and already infecting a population that had never expected to face such a thing again, Meru was not safe anywhere. None of the family was. Not Vekaa, not any of them.

Jian ran a broad range of web searches. Some would take time to complete, but the most direct queries yielded answers almost as soon as she asked the questions.

She called up a map of stars and worlds, stained blood red where the epidemic had already struck. Even while she had been in transit, the stain had expanded, the reach of the plague grown longer.

Shaking, fighting for focus, she called up another map, one that was keyed to her alone, and laid it over the other.

Her map showed a spread outward and then back, like a wave of the ocean that struck the shore and then withdrew. This new map, this The map of death came terribly close to completing it.

Her knees buckled. The floor of the dome rose to catch her.

Her mind at least was clear—the clarity of perfect terror. She left messages in places where the right people would find them, though not so quickly that any would be able to stop her. She let her staff and students know that she would be delayed in joining the expedition to the Caves of Song. Then she found a ship that would carry her to Earth.

The trail of the scarab led to the port city across from the island on which Jian had been born. She knew which ancient culture the bead had come from and roughly how old it was, but she still had no idea what it meant. There seemed to be no connection at all between a scarab from Egypt's Old Kingdom and an interstellar viral plague.

The person who had the original was a collector whom she had met before, an Earthling who traveled often offworld but kept a shop in the old city where he sold the occasional artifact. Not everything he dealt in was legal, but he had a good reputation. He was trustworthy, if not always careful to stay within the limits of a complex and sometimes contradictory code of law.

He had been away on one of his collecting expeditions, her sources told her, but had come back just a few days before. She took precautions: she made sure no one was following her either physically or on the web; she determined that all of the spybots around his shop were maintained or cleared by the collector himself. Finally she sent a message requesting entry, and received an answer keyed to her specific code: *Come.*

It seemed she was expected. Even so, she did not rush in all at once. She approached slowly, in clear view of the bots.

The shop's door opened as she came to it. She paused to run a scan. No weapons were trained on her. It was all open and honest as far as she could see.

She stepped inside.

The shop was deliberately, almost ostentatiously old-fashioned, in a style that was frankly ancient: dim, dark, cluttered. Instead of clean surfaces and virtual images that one selected from a range of menus, it was full of the actual artifacts.

Nothing there was particularly rare or valuable, but some of it was interesting. If Jian had had time, she would have loved to spend a few hours rummaging in the shelves and cabinets.

She could not spare those hours. She had seen a man sitting on a doorstep in a posture she recognized from too many worlds less blessed than Earth. He was sick. He was not one of the outcast, either—one of those who had been cut off, willingly or not, from the web. He was fully and properly protected, and the virus had taken all the strength out of his body.

She had the latest defenses, double-armored and fully charged. She would order them for Meru as soon as she finished here.

The collector was not in the shop, but he had left a message, a trail for her to follow. It led her to the back and up a stair to room as deliberately antique as the shop.

He was there, and he was dead. He had died quickly: he was sitting up with no sign of trauma, except for the blood trickling from his mouth and nostrils, ears and eyes.

The packet lay on the table beside him. Jian had come prepared: she carried a decontamination module. It flashed over the packet and signaled that it contained no threat.

Inside the packet was exactly what the data bead had promised: a scarab cupped in the mummy of a lotus blossom, resting on a scrap of papyrus that, from its shape, must once have been a wrapping for the rest. A stasis field prevented the fragile organic material from puffing to dust.

She ran the scan again, but this time she set it to detect and trace any viral contaminant. The search took so long that she had begun to sag in disappointment, sure that it had found nothing, when the scanner flashed.

The sample held nothing that the scanner considered dangerous, but there were slight anomalies. Those anomalies were little enough in themselves, but they hinted at something more.

It was maddening, because the traces were so faint, and yet there was no denying that they were there.

The collector had left a message for her on the shop's web. "I found this in a cache of artifacts on Alpha, last opened in the early years of the Lost Colony. I kept it because of your interest in that particular history. It seems a trivial thing to be so carefully preserved. Perhaps there is more to it than there seems to be."

Jian weighed the scarab in her hand. Trivial indeed.

And yet—it came from the Lost Colony. The first great plague of Earth's foray into space had destroyed every human being on that world.

This bead and this shadow of a flower had been there; had survived the plague and the cleansing that followed, the storm of fire that swept the planet down to the bare rock. To someone, for some reason she did not yet understand, this small thing had been immensely valuable.

Jian closed her eyes and sighed. She had been hoping to spend the night at home with her family—her daughter, her brother, all the aunts and uncles and cousins. But the hour was late and a storm was brewing, and suddenly she was tired. She had come a long way in search of an answer, only to find more questions.

Maybe there was no answer. Maybe it was all a preposterous prank, a joke played on her by one of her rivals, or a colleague with a twisted sense of humor.

She would know more tomorrow. And she would see Meru, which made her happy in spite of everything.

She took a room in a hostel nearby. By then her head ached dully; she was more than ready to sleep.

When she woke, she was dying. The being called Grey sat beside her.

She knew he was not real, because she could see through him. Her fever had conjured him up; the sickness gave him words to speak.

"Well done," he said. "Now wait. The rest will unfold as it must."

Waiting was one of the few things she could do at the moment, but she would be done with that all too soon. She would have told him so, if he had stayed.

Since he did not, she decontaminated the scarab and the flower yet again, even more carefully than before, and wrapped and sealed them and keyed the packet to Meru. She left it where she knew someone from Consensus would find it.

She hoped it would be Vekaa. He was as close to a disease specialist as Earth still had.

When that was done, she set her implants to record her memories of Grey and of the scarab, and to finish the recording here, soon, as the life left her body.

She had done all she could. Probably she had done more than she should.

She appreciated the irony. The plague she had hunted for so long had caught her at last, just as she came within reach of proving her theory. If there were still gods anywhere in the universe, they must be amused.

Jian's mind was breaking up; her streams of data were running dry. She tried to reach Meru, to tell her—something; anything. But her grip on the world had let go.

The data stream broke apart as Jian's mind had done, disintegrating into fragments of random information. It was dead, gone, erased, everywhere on the web. But it was burned into Meru's memory.

Meru lay in the light of a million suns, with tears running down her face.

Yoshi's head blocked a fraction of the light. She could not make out his expression: the stars were too bright. But his voice was, as usual, worried. "Are you all right? What happened?"

"I have got to stop doing things that make you ask that," she said.

"That would be good," he said. "But since you've done it again, will you please tell me what's wrong this time?"

Meru could not decide whether to laugh or sob. The sound that came out could have passed for either or both. "I found what I needed to find. What my mother did. Why she—why she died." She stopped, breathed, made herself go on steadily. "There's one last thing I have to do. Since there's no way I'm going to be able to talk you out of coming with me, will you just come? And not argue?"

He dropped down from above her, so that finally she could see his face. It was tired and drawn and amazingly, incongruously happy. She could hardly help herself: she touched it, as if to assure herself that it was real.

It was. He was. "When are we going?" he asked.

He was as crazy as Meru.

As he would be. He wanted to be a starpilot, too.

# Meritre

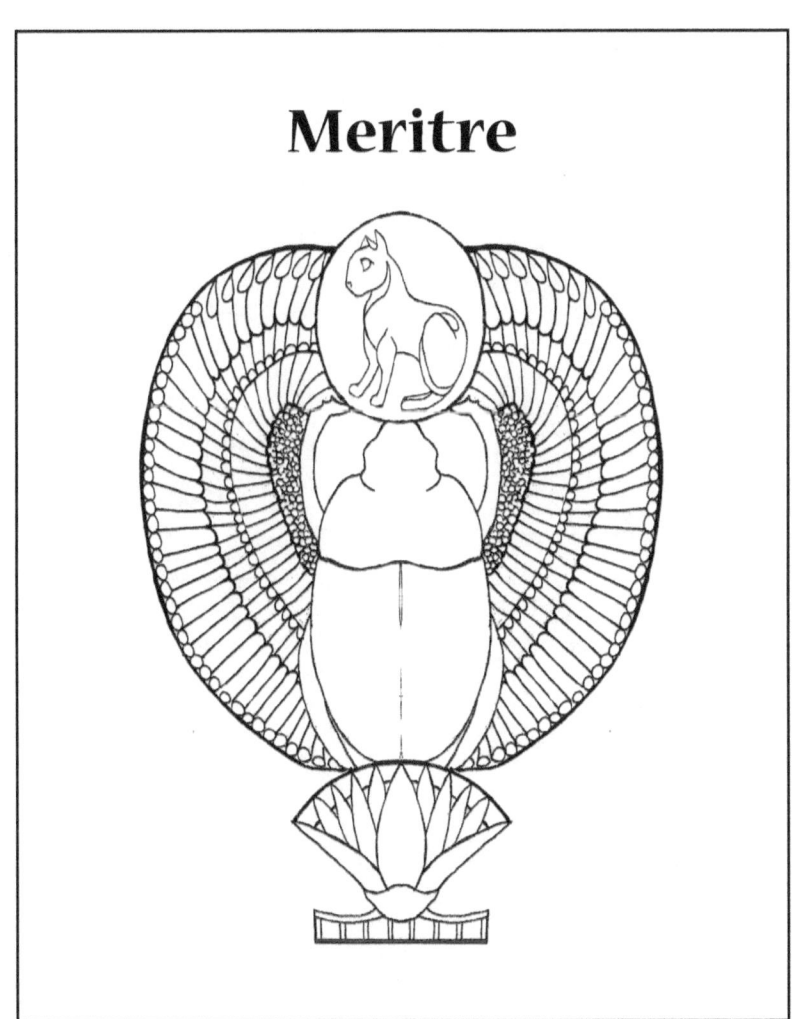

# Chapter 21

Meritre felt strange. The spirits that had been inside her were gone, cut off by Meredith's will. What she felt, she realized as she watched the sun come up over the city, was loneliness. She was alone inside herself, as every human thing was supposed to be—and it felt deeply and painfully wrong.

She was not angry at Meredith. People did what they did; and Meredith had had a terrible shock. But Meritre did wish her other self had chosen a better time. Meru's people needed knowledge that Meritre had, or could get. Now there was no way to pass that knowledge to her.

Meritre could surrender and fall back into her old, ordinary life. Or she could do something. It might not be of any use, but at least she would have tried.

Her blue bead, her simple and unremarkable scarab, seemed to be the key to the spell that bound them all. Meredith had said that her people had found it somewhere Meritre was unlikely ever to go: in a passage below the princess' temple.

Meritre would go to the temple. The gods might speak to her if she did that, or she might see where the tomb was. She might even find a way to tell Meru without Meredith to carry the words onward.

It was worth doing. Certainly it was better than fretting uselessly at home.

Her father was to work in the temple today. He had to finish carving and painting the statue there before it was put in place in the tomb.

She was not foolish enough to ask him where the tomb was hidden. He would not answer; he was sworn to silence. But she knew a way.

She managed to distract him enough with fuss and chatter that when he left the house, he forgot the basket of bread and beer that should have been his morning meal. Someone had to take it to him or he would be hungry all day.

Meritre had made sure she had to be that someone. Her brothers were busy in the king's workshop. Aweret was feeling the weight of the baby and needed to rest.

By the time Meritre reached the river, the ferry was nearly full. That was almost enough to convince her that the gods did not approve of her plan. But her father needed to eat, and Meru's world needed much more than that. She balanced the basket on her head and squeezed in among the crowd.

Most of them were mourners going to visit their relatives among the tombs. They were a big family, not wealthy enough to own their own ferry, but much sleeker and better dressed than Meritre.

Some of the younger men eyed her with clear intention. She kept her own eyes bent downward.

When one of the men moved toward her, she measured paths of escape. There were not many, and most of those were also occupied by well-fed young men.

A clear voice rang above the murmur of conversation. "Khafre! Come here and hold my sunshade."

The man with the wandering feet stopped short. Meritre had to crane a bit to see through the thicket of bodies, but after a moment she saw who had spoken: a woman who must be Khafre's mother or aunt, seated on a chair that must have been brought for just that purpose. She looked as high and haughty as one might expect, noblewoman that she clearly was.

But as her eye caught Meritre's, there was something else in it. A surprising warmth; a flicker of sympathy.

She reminded Meritre of the king, a little. Meritre bowed to her, slightly but visibly.

And she bowed back. That left Meritre feeling somewhat off balance, but somehow, out of nowhere in particular, rather ridiculously happy.

It could be an omen, if she chose to see it as such. She hugged its memory to her as the ferry touched the bank and the crowd jostled and chattered its way toward the harsh beauty of the Red Land.

She had never been across the river where the dead were. Her father had gone there sometimes to work on tombs, as he did now, and Aweret had gone in processions, singing a late king or a king's wife into eternity. Meritre would do that for the princess when the time of embalming was over.

Today she had a different errand, one she could not have explained to anyone. She balanced her basket on her head again and walked up from the landing, following the track that led toward the cliffs.

No one else was going where she was going. After such a crowd, even with predators in it, she felt very much alone under the vault of the sky.

The sun was well on its way toward the zenith by the time Meritre made her way up the last steep ascent into the valley where the queens were buried. The king would have liked to build her heir's home for eternity among the kings, but some things in this world, even a king knew better than to try.

Sounds of hammering and grinding and shouts of workmen echoed down the track long before Meritre had climbed far enough to see the temple. It had gone up almost overnight, but it looked well made, with tall columns and smooth paving and statues of the king on either side of the entrance.

There was scaffolding up against the left-hand statue. Men perched on it, painting the king's headdress in stripes of blue and gold.

One of the artists painting the inscriptions down below pointed Meritre toward the place where her father was working. There were guards everywhere; they did not offer to help, but they did not try to stop her, either.

The painter's directions took her to the back of the temple and then out onto a sort of porch, where masons and sculptors worked in the shade of a canopy. Meritre found her father almost at once.

The statue was nearly done; it was so lifelike it made her stop short, though it was no taller than a newborn baby. That was the princess' face to the life, with its round cheeks and soft mouth. He was painting it with such skill that it seemed almost to breathe.

Meritre waited until he paused and straightened, setting the brush down. He stretched, frowned and then smiled as he saw Meritre. "You forgot this," she said, lowering the basket from her head and holding it out to him.

"You came a long way," he said as he took the basket and dived into his breakfast. "Does your mother know you're here?"

"Yes," said Meritre. "She didn't want you to go hungry all day."

He grunted. "And you were curious. Weren't you?"

"Well," she said, "yes."

"You'll pay for that," he said. "I'm not letting you go back alone. You'll stay here till we're done, then we'll take the ferry back together."

Meritre hoped she managed to conceal the surge of relief when he said that. She had been avoiding the issue of how she was going to get back to the city, but that took care of it. It gave her half the day to do what she had come to do.

The gods were with her. She should never have doubted it.

"Here," he said, passing her one of the jars of beer. "Drink up, but take your time. You'll be here for a while."

She nodded, wide-eyed. His glance was suspicious, but the statue was waiting, and it had to be done before the princess came back from the embalmers. In a breath's space he was engrossed in his work again.

When she slipped away, she more than half expected him to call her back. But he had forgotten her. No one else seemed to care what she did. The guards were all in the front of the temple, making sure no one got in from the road or the river.

The tomb had to be somewhere nearby. She would expect it to be under heavy guard, but except for the workers in the temple and the guards at the gate, the valley was deserted.

She wandered back into the temple. The part she was in was finished, except for an artist working on inscriptions in a passageway that sloped down from the north side of the temple. He bent close to the wall a handful of man-lengths down the passage, tracing the shapes of hieroglyphs with a steady hand. Meritre gambled that he would be as oblivious as her father, and slipped past him on silent feet.

"Meritre?"

She knew that voice. She stopped and spun. Djehuti looked up at her from where he knelt on the floor.

"What are you doing here?" she demanded.

His lips twitched. "You're always asking me that."

"Really," she said. "Aren't you supposed to be working with the king's scribes?"

"Usually I am," he said, "but the king wrote this, and she wanted it written here."

"Why?"

He set his lips together.

Meritre knew a secret when she saw one. She bent and peered at the line he had already painted. It was a poem, a verse that told of a mother's love for her child.

She stood up straight. When she moved, she saw something odd. The floor slanted slightly but distinctly downward. The passage went on into darkness, much farther than she had expected.

Might this be...?

The gods were here, watching her. She could feel them. She took a deep breath and let it out, and laid it all in their hands. "This is it, isn't it? This is the way to the tomb."

She watched Djehuti make up his mind to lie, but then change it when his eyes met hers. He must feel it, too: the gods' hands on them both. "Yes," he said. "You know you'll die if you tell anyone."

"I know," she said. She moved past him down the passage.

There was no light but the little that came from the chapel, and Djehuti had bolted. He was going for the guards after all.

As he should. Why did it hurt so much? He was just a boy she liked to look at, and sometimes talk to. He was not betraying anything that had honestly been between them. He was saving his life and livelihood, and doing his duty.

She should run back to the sculptors' porch before the guards came, but she had come too far to give up. She kept on going.

Light flickered behind her. She flattened against the wall.

There was only one shadow, leaping and dancing. Djehuti had a torch, and he was alone.

Meritre could die here if that was his intention, and it would be days before anyone found her. But as she peered up the tunnel at the shadowy blur of his face, she knew he had not come to kill her. Nor had he betrayed her.

"You don't have to do this," she said.

"I know." He brought the torch up beside her. She could smell the oil in it, and the hot smell of the flame. "It's farther than you might think."

"Really," she said. "You don't. Just let me have the torch. If I'm caught, and anyone asks, I stole it myself."

"It's not stolen," he said. "I need light to work. And to look over what I've done already, in case of mistakes. The whole spell could fail for the lack of a single glyph."

"That...is a good story."

"It happens to be true." He raised the torch slightly, so that she could see the painted words marching away into the shadows. "Would you like to see?"

"Am I supposed to?"

"No," he said. "But you were intending to, weren't you? What have you seen?"

"I'm not a performing ape!"

He swayed in the wind of her outburst. She clapped her hands over her mouth.

When the echoes were well and truly dead, she lowered her hands. Djehuti stood still, steady on his feet, slightly wide-eyed.

"I am sorry," she said. "I don't know where that came from."

"I understand," he said. "If you can't tell me—if the gods want you to keep the secret—"

It would be easy to let him think that was true. And in its way it was. But she owed him something more, for what he was doing for her, and for the price he might have to pay for it.

"I need to see the tomb," she said. "Just see it. Not touch, or tell—not in this age of the world. That I promise you. I will take the secret to my own tomb."

She held her breath. If he asked what she meant, she was not sure she could answer.

He frowned. She braced herself. After a moment he said, "Scribes have secrets, too. And magic doesn't always make sense outside of itself."

He was talking to himself, she thought, more than to her. Reciting a lesson, maybe. Making a decision.

Finally he said, "Follow me."

The breath ran out of her so fast she nearly fell.

He was there, catching her hand, holding her up. His grip was warm and strong. His trust was even stronger. What it meant…

What was between two people did not always make sense out of itself, either. Still hand in hand, they descended toward the tomb.

It was a long way under the earth, down the slowly slanting shaft that was just a little higher than Djehuti's head. There had been no time to paint any of the walls there; everything that anyone could do had to be done in the tomb itself, down deep where, gods willing, the grave robbers would be less likely to find and strip it.

Grave robbers were like rats in a granary. One did all one could to keep them out, but if there was any possible way in, they would find it.

Djehuti had done what he could to help, painting curses and strong spells on the walls and door of the deep chamber. The niche where Father's statue of the *ka* would go was finished and painted to look like a room in a house, with a window showing a garden of palms and fruit trees. When the statue went into it, it would be walled up, all but the narrow door that would let the *ka* go back and forth.

Meritre shivered. It was almost cold down here, as if the spells on the walls and door had drained the heat out of the air. She bowed and murmured a prayer to the gods who hovered all around her, invisible but clearly perceptible.

The torch had begun to flicker. Without a word spoken, they both turned and walked quickly away from the tomb.

When they were halfway up the long ascent, they heard voices ahead. There was no way out but the one, and no side path, no room to hide in. All they could do was go forward and hope they could talk their way out of it.

Meritre's heart was beating so hard she was sure the people outside could hear it. Even when the voices passed, she could not force herself to be calm.

Djehuti edged ahead of her. The torch had almost burned out. He stopped and stood listening.

After a long count of heartbeats he nodded, stubbed out the torch against the floor, and strode quickly toward the glimmer of daylight at the end of the tunnel.

Meritre hesitated. The darkness around her was thick and strangely cool. Djehuti's painted images glowed ahead of her.

Without stopping to think, with a gesture as inevitable as the advance of time through thousands of years, she slipped off the amulet that her mother had given her when she was tiny, knelt down and laid it on the floor. She heard the faint clatter and the barely audible sound of the bead rolling toward the wall.

She felt naked without it, and her heart wrenched. She might never talk to her other selves again now she had let go the key to the spell.

She had to. Otherwise Meredith would never find it, and it would not come to Meru.

The spell was set. She had made her sacrifice. She could go; she could return to the world of the living.

Djehuti knelt where she had found him when she first came. He picked up his brush just as a pair of guards strolled past the chapel. They hardly deigned to notice the workman in the passage, or the flushed and tousled girl who held his palette for him. If they thought anything, Meritre could all too easily imagine what it was.

It was worth the price. Djehuti was, too, she thought, turning her mind deliberately away from thousands and thousands of years, toward the future that was directly ahead of her. A future, she thought, that she would like him to keep on being part of.

She caught him glancing at her. His ears were slightly but distinctly red. He was blushing. She wanted to laugh—but her ears felt as hot as his.

# Meredith

# Chapter 22

My world was breaking apart. I needed to be alone. Completely alone—all by myself, with no one yammering at me, inside my head or out.

I felt guilty, of course I did. Meru's world was literally breaking, and she'd already lost the person who mattered the most to her. But I couldn't help. I could barely help myself.

I should march out of my room and face down Dad and Aunt Jessie and Kelly and make them tell me the truth. I meant to. I just couldn't bring myself to start.

I lay on the bed and stared at the knot of mosquito netting directly above me. I'd been crying off and on. Mostly off, now. My throat was raw. I was sick to my stomach.

Part of me kept spinning the story that might be real and might be absolute craziness. In that story, time was getting short. The princess' tomb wasn't going anywhere, any more than it had for the past four thousand years.

But I had this inescapable feeling that we had to find it now, and not wait till the next digging season, or whenever Aunt Jessie could get back here. The connection, the Triple, wasn't so much like three points on a line as three wires twisted around each other. We were beads on those wires, and our beads were touching. If one moved, they all moved. If one refused...

My now and Meritre's now and Meru's now were happening, well, *now*. And I was the big fat wrench in the works.

Time-travel stories always gave me a migraine. Now I was trapped in one. I hadn't written any stories of my own since I started slipping in and out of the past and the future.

I had my tablet in bed, with a book I'd been not-reading for I don't know how many days. My laptop was shut down and my phone was buried in my knapsack, but when the tablet pinged, I remembered I'd forgotten to turn the wi-fi off. That meant Skype was on, and instead of a screen of text, I was glaring at a blurry, pixilated, and totally familiar face topped with a halo of short purple spikes.

"Ha!" said Cat. "Caught you. Where have you been? What's wrong?"

She sounded so much like Yoshi and Djehuti that I almost let out a howl. Damn. Were we *all* cursed with people who cared about us?

"Hey," said Cat. "Talk to me. Everybody else is going on about how you're busy and you're on the other side of the world and who has time for the folks back home any more. Except Rick. You know him. He just says you'll get around to it when you get around to it."

That was Rick. I didn't mean to burst into tears again. God, no. But I couldn't stop once I started.

Cat got it. Cat always got it—even when she only had a fraction of the data. "It's your mom, isn't it?"

Funny thing about meltdowns. Sometimes they go all Fukushima. And sometimes you find bedrock. Like when you've got a friend looking at you on a tablet screen from six thousand miles away.

I wished I could touch her. Just for a second. Just to feel the warmth, and be close to something real and solid and human.

"It's Mom," I said. "She's in hospice. They didn't tell me. They shipped me out and they didn't—tell—"

"Bastards."

Cat's voice was cold murder. It made me yelp. "Don't kill anybody!"

"I'm not ready for humans yet," she said. "I can't even pass the torturing-animals phase. I look into their little eyes and go all squooshy."

"You are a miserable failure as a serial killer," I said. My eyes were still trying to run over, but Cat had me laughing, even if it was a horrible bad excuse for a funny.

"Do you need me to go over to the hospice?" Cat asked. "Not to commit any violence. Just to, you know, find out for sure?"

I felt tension running out of me that I hadn't even known was there. "I would like that," I said. Then it all came rushing back. "But will they let you in?"

"I'll figure it out," she said. "You go dig up mummies. I'll get the truth about your mom."

She didn't even know how close she was to the rest of what was wrong with me. I almost broke down again, but I managed to hold on. "Thanks, Cat."

"You'd do the same for me," she said. "Don't worry, okay? Or not any more than you absolutely have to."

Weird how a three-minute Skype can change the whole way you look at the world. I didn't feel all that much better, and the tears still came and went, but my mind was working again.

Being my mind, what it was doing was figuring out how to get at the princess' tomb. Not necessarily because I wanted to help Meru. Just because I wanted to know.

If I was going to do it, I'd figure out a way to get Aunt Jessie down into the tunnel in the morning. Then I'd get creative and convince her not to take days opening the door.

If I'd been in an adventure story as well as a time-travel story, I'd have sneaked out, stolen a boat, and done my own excavating that night. But that was stupid. It was also gawdawful archaeology.

I couldn't sleep. I kept jumping awake, thinking I'd heard a ping from the tablet, and Cat was calling and she was with Mom and Mom was back home and it was all just a false alarm.

There wasn't any ping. Cat didn't call. Neither did Mom.

When the cat scratched and mewped at the door, I let her in. She jumped up on the bed and purred next to me until I fell into a twitchy doze.

After all that, I almost missed the alarm. The cat took care of it for me. She laid a paw against my face and ever so gently flexed it.

That woke me up. She butted her head against my chin and purred so loud it made my head rattle. I staggered into the shower, then down to breakfast.

I almost didn't go to the site. I could say I hadn't slept, which was true, and I was sick, which was close enough to true. I could go on hiding. Maybe I could hide so long and well, I completely disappeared.

I wasn't that smart, or that lucky. I went through the motions I went through every morning, as if the world was still the same place it had been yesterday and the day before.

By the time we lurched onto the ferry, I was most of the way awake. Dad and Kelly weren't with us today. I hadn't said a word to Aunt Jessie. I was afraid that if I did, I'd start screaming; or worse, I'd start crying again.

My half-crazy plans to find the tomb had evaporated with the daylight. What did I need it for, anyway? It wouldn't do Mom any good.

If I'd been thinking, I would have buried myself in the tent with the latest box of potsherds. I followed Aunt Jessie instead. Apart from a glance I couldn't read, she didn't say anything.

She always checked on the tunnel crew first before she went to whichever part of the site she felt needed her most. The crew was down there already. I'd thought they were supposed to stop where they left off yesterday, but either someone didn't get the memo or they'd decided to give it one last try.

Maybe Aunt Jessie had a feeling. What I had was 'way more than that, even without the other two riding inside my head.

The sound of chipping and scraping came up from below. They must have found the clues I'd left.

When we got there, there were just three men working, including Sayyid the foreman. They'd opened up a bit more from where I'd been with the trowel last night, then started in higher, right about face height. Sayyid was working away at the bricks.

He looked back when he heard us. Aunt Jessie raised her eyebrows at him. "Anything?"

"Maybe," he said. "Maybe not. Have a look."

She moved in beside him, took his hammer and chisel and started chipping. She wasn't in any hurry. Her hands weren't shaking. But she was working fast.

One of the workmen brought a face mask for her, and one for me, too. The whole thing about the curse of the pharaohs—that's just crap. But there are things that live in tombs and other places that have been closed in for thousands of years, molds and bacteria—viruses, too, maybe—that can kill anybody who plows in without protection.

The mask was hot and confining, but I made myself put up with it. I wanted to go on breathing after we got done here.

I wasn't coherent enough to be excited. I had to see, that was all. I had to know.

While Aunt Jessie worked away at the bricks, the foreman fiddled with a metal case. The others were watching. Nobody was talking. You know how they say you can feel tension in the air? This was thick enough to cut like butter.

Aunt Jessie worked a brick free. Sayyid finally got the case open and took out what was inside.

It was a camera. It had a long snaky coil that could go down drains or into rubble after an earthquake or a building collapse—or into a tomb.

Nobody ripped walls out any more until they knew what was inside. They couldn't officially do that anyway without permission from the Board of Antiquities—and for this, I would bet pretty much anything that the Director would insist on being here when it happened.

What we were doing now was just this side of legal. We had to look, right? We had to be sure this wasn't another blind alley.

Aunt Jessie looked over her shoulder at me. "Come here."

I could hardly breathe, and not just because of the mask. This was the moment every Egyptologist prayed for. And she was sharing it with me.

I suppose it was an apology. I didn't know about accepting it—some things you can't just pay off with the discovery of the century. But I wasn't turning it down, either.

Aunt Jessie's hand gripped my arm. It held me together.

"Don't get your hopes up," she said. "There could be nothing on the other side but empty space."

"If that's what's there, at least we'll know."

She nodded. She was wound tight, but she was keeping it under control.

While Aunt Jessie set up the camera, I stood on tiptoe and peered through the hole. I didn't expect to see anything. It would be pitch black in there.

The way the lights were hung, one shone right past me. I looked straight into a pair of heavily painted Egyptian eyes.

I'm not a screamer or a fainter. I freeze. By the time my heart stopped hammering so hard I was afraid it would shake itself right out of my chest, I realized what it had to be. I was looking into the niche where the *ka* statue stood.

It was doll-sized—maybe two feet high. It looked exactly the way it had when Meritre was alive, yesterday, four thousand years ago.

I stepped back carefully. I wanted to say something, but there weren't any words.

I shivered. The tunnel had been hot and close with all of us in it, but now it was cool again. It felt almost cold.

Maybe it's true what I've heard, that when ghosts are walking through, they take the heat out of the air. Though if there was a ghost here now, who was it? The princess? Or Meritre?

Maybe it was me. I was dead, too, in Meru's time.

Aunt Jessie got the camera working. I had to move over so she could thread it through the hole.

There was enough space for me to stand next to her and see the screen. I had a flash, a memory of standing with Bonnie, watching Dr. Kay do the ultrasound. It felt pretty much the same. Breathless. Hoping. Not hoping. Praying, maybe.

At first there was just a blur: a wall, a fuzz of color that was the statue, another wall—that one was painted all over, everywhere. Then there was brightness.

Gold. It didn't matter what shape it took. It was there.

Robbers didn't leave that much gold in a tomb. This was what Tut's tomb was like—why it was so incredible. It hadn't been robbed.

The camera caught on something and stopped moving. Pure luck, if there is any such thing, put it at just the right angle to see the length of the tomb.

It was a vault with painted walls and a ceiling covered with stars. The sarcophagus filled most of the middle. It was hard to tell how big it was.

Big. That much we had to figure. But the amazing thing, the incredible thing, even more than the golden treasure that lay everywhere, was the flowers.

The place was full of them, piled on the floor around the hoard and heaped up around the sarcophagus. A carpet of them lay over the top of it.

They'd withered—in four thousand years, that was hardly a surprise. Deep inside, cut off from the air, they'd kept their color. They looked as if they'd been picked yesterday.

As soon as the tomb opened, they'd puff to dust. We were the only ones who would see them the way they'd been left.

"Organic material."

I started. My eyes darted everywhere. Then I realized. It was Meru's voice. She was back inside my head.

So was Meritre. "Oh!" she said. "*Oh!* We don't need the scarab. I was so afraid—I thought—"

"Maybe at first," Meru said, "but not any more. We know what we are. That's all we need."

That, and me in the middle. With the tomb in front of me, and all those beautiful, impossible flowers, I'd forgotten to keep blocking the others out.

"Beautiful, deadly flowers," Meru said. "Masses of them. A body underneath, riddled with infection. But how could it survive eight thousand years? In ice, maybe, but in dry heat and after seventy days of embalming?"

"That would have to be one determined virus," I said in my head. I was glad I had a mask on—though if this was as bad as Meru thought it was, a full hazmat suit wouldn't be enough.

I stopped that thought before I ran off screaming.

"Even supposing this is where the plague came from," Meru said, "it must have had to mutate, probably a lot more than once, after it got loose. That mutation couldn't have happened in your time, or Consensus would know about it and be able to stop it. You should be safe."

"You hope," I said.

While I carried on the conversation with the voices in my head,

Sayyid and the two workmen took turns looking at the camera image. Their eyes were huge, and I could hear how fast they were breathing, but nobody said a word. It was like a pact—literal silence.

Finally Aunt Jessie reeled the camera back in. She put the brick back, too. She wasn't hiding anything. Just keeping the air out—or in.

"You know we can't talk about this." She said it to me. She must figure no one else needed to be told.

I didn't either, but I didn't try to argue. I stood there and let her finish her speech. "We have to keep this a secret for now. We'll call the Director of Antiquities and let him know what we've found. He gets to decide when and how the tomb is opened. It could be a media circus—or he might keep it quiet for a while. It's up to him."

I nodded. We were all holding ourselves in tight, including the Triple: Meritre because this was tomb robbery no matter what we called it, and Meru because the answers were here, and she was starting to understand what they were.

My time was important for archaeologists—transitional, Meru's sources on the web said. We still opened tombs, but we'd stopped shoving mummies in boxes and hauling them off to foreign museums. Once a tomb was investigated and catalogued, the mummy went back in, along with most of the things it had been buried with. Which meant that in Meru's time, it might be still there, and still all or mostly intact.

Meanwhile, in my time, we tried to act as if nothing had happened. Sayyid left the men down there on guard. Aunt Jessie went to supervise the other half of the dig, around the porch where Meritre had seen the sculptors working.

I had potsherds to label and a life to try not to think about. Mom's life. Mine, because my relatives were arguing over what to do with me, and I didn't seem to have a say in it.

I'd rather think about the tomb that we'd found. The incredible, amazing, wonderful discovery that when it finally got out, would make the world fall in love with Egypt all over again.

The discovery that, four thousand years from now, would be killing people—somehow. Meru was hunting down the cause now, then, whatever. In my head, she was doing it at the same time as I was pasting numbers on beads and amulets and pieces of pottery.

I hoped she found it. After all the drama I'd put us through, I wanted to know. This was our project, cause, fate, destiny—pick a word, it probably applied. We were all in it together.

# Meru

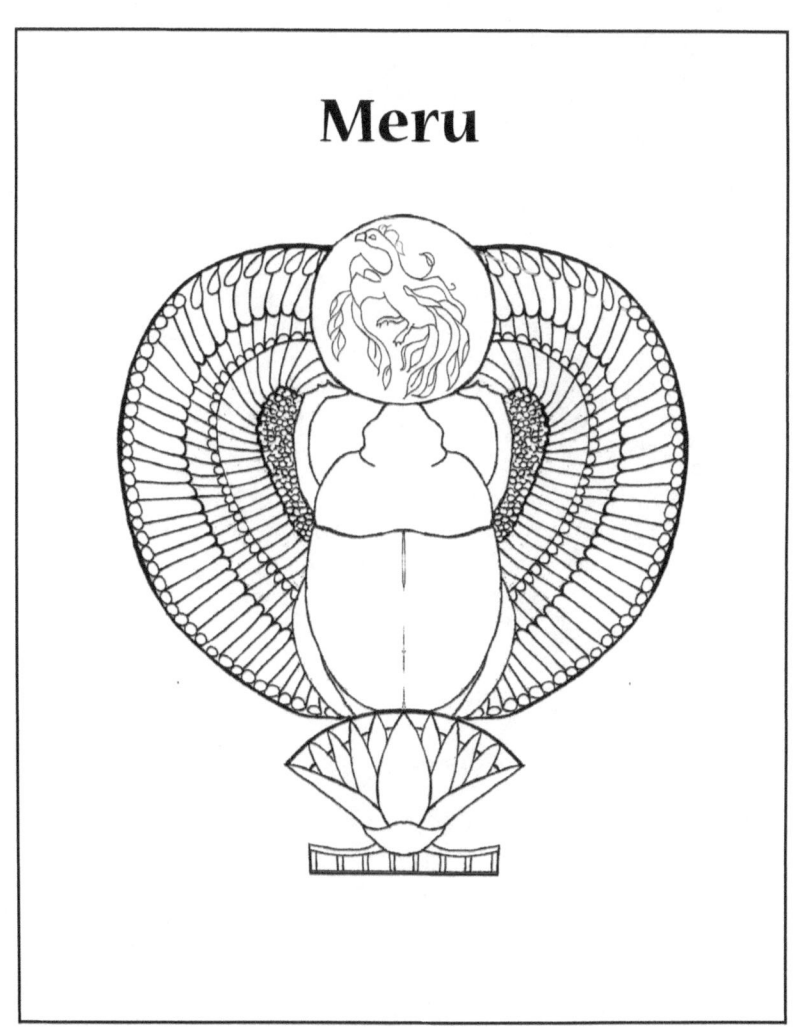

# Chapter 23

I've got it," Meru said. "I know where we're going. Or," she added, "mostly."

"Let me see," Yoshi said.

She sent him what she had, which was a map of Egypt as Meredith remembered it. While he pondered that, she skimmed along the newsfeed—and stopped.

*Sixteen deaths in the past Earthday in SudAfrique. Forty-three in Eurasia. And in NorthAm—*

"Seventy-nine," Meru said, "that Consensus will admit to. But the real numbers—"

"People aren't stupid," Yoshi said. "They can count. They share links. Consensus can't keep hiding this."

The toll was rising. No one dared use the word yet, but it hung above them all. *Pandemic.*

Meru shut off the feed before it shut down her courage. She closed her eyes, the better to see what Meredith had given her. With that to draw on, she could map the world. She traced the rise and fall of seas and the shifting of land masses until she found what she was looking for.

"That's it?" Yoshi said, far out on the edge of the web. "That's where it is?"

"That's it," Meru said.

It was still a fiercely hot place, and the river still ran through it, though its course had changed and changed again in all those thousands of years. The desert had turned to jungle and then back to desert, but the ancient monuments were still there, preserved for eternity. That pleased Meritre.

For the second time in her life, Meru packed what she needed for an escape. It was not so easy this time. The house was under lockdown, and she was under surveillance.

That would not matter so much if it had not been for Yoshi. "I don't suppose I can possibly convince you to stay here after all?" she said.

He set his mouth in a line. "No."

"Not even as a diversion? To cover for me? To—"

"No."

"You can't help," she said. "You'll only hinder."

"You don't know that," he said. "If you try to web-tie me and run away, I'll hack myself out and go after you. You can't do this alone. You need backup."

"I *have*—" Meru broke off. If she had to explain the Triple, she would be there all night.

"All right," she said, and she was not happy about it at all. "Stay close. Stay quiet. And no questions."

He opened his mouth. She glared. He shut it. "Let's go," he said.

The house was on lockdown. As free as Meru was of the web, she was confined physically as everyone else was, until Consensus lifted the ban.

Consensus had not factored in the starwing. Meru was not entirely sure of it, either; she could only ask.

It had been basking in starlight, purring to itself. When she called, it ignored her.

She thrust down the stab of fear and the crippling disappointment, and willed herself to be calm. It was not her tool or her slave, after all. It was a living being.

"Please," she said to it. "Will you help?"

It spread its wings and trilled. Its focus was not on her; it was on the field that surrounded the house, the beautiful, delicious, intoxicating energy that fed it until it was crackling all over.

She turned away. She would not let herself be hurt, or feel betrayed.

There was another thing she could do, which might fail terribly. Or it might succeed. Either way, it was better than giving up; than doing nothing.

Vekaa was in the common room with the family. They were all there, from the eldest to the youngest, and they were in the middle of an argument.

"We have no objection to confining ourselves to the house," Grandmother Ramotswe said, "or to observing proper precautions during this, as you put it, *situation*. But we want our daughter's body back."

"You will get it back," Vekaa said, "when the situation has calmed down."

"We understand that," said Grandmother Ramotswe. "We also understand that it will have to be thoroughly and conclusively decontaminated. But what you propose to do with it—"

"Those were her wishes," Vekaa said. "She asked that once her genetic material was taken and recorded, her ashes be scattered among the stars."

"I'm sure," said Grandmother Ramotswe, "but she was a member of this family. And members of this family rest in the vault beneath the house. She belongs here. Not out there, drifting with the interstellar dust."

"We are all made of interstellar dust," Meru said. She had meant to be quiet, but she could not help herself. "The stars are in every one of us. Does it matter where she is? Her genetic code is here. Her memory lives in all of us. Why can't what's left of her go where she wanted it to go?"

"It's not done," Uncle Goro said. "It's never been done."

"Then maybe it's time it was," said Vekaa.

He walked out on them. Meru stood with the rest, staring at the door through which he had vanished.

Almost too late she remembered how to think, and then to move. Yoshi was already in motion. Meru stretched her stride to pass him.

Vekaa had not gone far. He was in the room he liked to sleep in; Yoshi caught and held the door before he could seal it.

He regarded them wearily. "Yes," he said to Meru, "I should have called you down for that."

"You should," she said. "But it doesn't matter. Not for now." She drew a breath and let it out, all at once. "I know where to find the key to the plague. Will you help me get there?"

Was that hope in his face? Or was he too tired to feel anything? "I don't know if I have that power," he said.

"The Deciders do." Meru said. She was proud of herself for saying it so calmly.

"There are procedures," he said. "Protocols. I don't know if—"

"So more people will die because it takes too long to make a decision?"

"Consensus takes time," he said.

"You don't believe that yourself," she said. "I can tell. You won't look at me when you say it. You were supposed to have gone to your laboratory after you locked me up here. What happened? Did you leave?"

"No," said Vekaa. "I…was put on leave. For refusing consensus. For arguing in favor of my sister's thoroughly and conclusively discredited theories."

"But they're true," Meru said. "She was right."

"You can prove it?"

"I know where to find proof."

He unfolded slowly, as if his bones hurt. She looked hard at him, holding back terror.

He did not look sick. Only exhausted.

Could she tell the difference?

"I still have some of my clearances," he said. "They may be enough."

"If you have them down to the third level," said Yoshi, "I can take them the rest of the way." He flushed as they both turned on him. "I haven't done anything illegal! Often. Much. One of my uncles is a coordinator in Transport. I used to watch him when he worked."

"And you paid attention," Meru said.

"I'd get bored," he said. "It was all there was to do."

"Do it," said Vekaa, "but let me monitor."

"And me," said Meru.

Yoshi spread his hands. "Why not? We're all going down to together anyway."

"I hope not," Meru said.

Meru was very good at hacking the web, but Yoshi was an artist. Vekaa's clearances made his avatar dance with glee. Still dancing, he drew in the threads of sites and connections so quickly that Meru could barely keep up.

He mapped a route and secured a bubble and a shuttle, with clearances that would pass them invisibly through Containment—and he left a ping for the Deciders, but set it to reach them after the three of them had arrived in what once was Egypt. It was better than hiding in plain sight: it was perfectly open and transparent, but by the time Consensus knew what they were doing, they would have finished doing it.

"Clever," Vekaa said. Meru could not tell if he approved.

"You're not going to stop us, are you?" she asked.

"Could I?"

"No," she admitted.

"So then." He inspected the order for the bubble, and raised a brow. "That's clever, too: summoning it for Family Nkomo. Do you realize how far that is from here?"

"It's not too far to walk," Yoshi said.

Vekaa rather carefully did not say anything.

"*I* can walk that far," said Yoshi. "Are you coming?"

It might not be far, but it was hard going. Meru was not used to walking on raw earth, clambering over rocks and slipping on patches of ice. She took some solace from the fact that the others were struggling even more than she was—especially Yoshi, whose brilliance had brought them to this place.

As soon as they had slipped and clambered out of sight of the house, the starwing came floating down out of the sky, singing a sweet and faintly drunken song. Its wings were shimmering with auroras.

It wrapped itself around Meru. She was floating; flying. Swimming in cold fire.

She could have lost herself in the sheer giddy joy of it. But people were dying. She had to extricate herself; to set her feet on the hard, cold track and lead her uncle and her friend toward the bubble.

The starwing shrank to its smallest size and perched on her shoulder. She had not realized how much she missed it until she had it back again. Its soft trilling in her ear muted the whine of the wind. Its weightless presence made her feet light, even if she would not let it lift her above it all and carry her into the sky.

Yoshi slipped and slid and went tumbling past her down the rock-strewn slope. He fetched up against the stump of a tree.

Meru skidded toward him in a fit of pure white panic. He lay crumpled, legs sprawling. He was not breathing. He was not—

He twitched. Wheezed. "What—"

She pulled him to his feet. He wobbled, then steadied. "Don't *do* that!" she snapped at him.

She was shaking him. She made herself stop. Breathe. Think—which was hardest of all. "Can you walk?"

He was stiff and his left ankle was not bending quite as it should, but it got better as he moved. He looked up at Vekaa, who had come down much more cautiously, and said, "Next time I'll try not to be so clever."

"One hopes there will be no next time," Vekaa said dryly.

Between them, Meru and Vekaa half-carried, half-supported Yoshi back up the slope and toward the track. Time ticked away while they struggled with the ice and the stones. Yoshi had far underestimated how much of it they would need.

He had miscalculated where the road was, too. Distances on foot were nothing like distances by bubble or walkway.

Meritre, who knew feet and boats, showed Meru how to keep a long and steady stride, even up steep hillsides and down rocky escarpments. It needed balance and confidence, and a great deal of patience.

Meru could not let herself panic over how long it was taking. The bubble would wait. Yoshi had put a hold on it.

The longer it waited, the more likely it was that Consensus would find it. She had to put that thought out of her mind, too.

When at long last they came to the road, there was nothing on it. Meru started to sag in defeat—then she saw the shimmer hovering just above the silvery surface.

The bubble was under full security. When she came to stand in front of it, it flickered into visibility.

She had never been so grateful to see a transport bubble in her life. Yoshi acted for them all when he blew a kiss at it. He limped on board under his own power, and dropped with a blissful groan to the soft, warm floor.

When the bubble began to move, it moved much more quickly than any Meru had been in before. "Consensus-level clearance," Yoshi said a little smugly.

"Sixth level?" Vekaa shook his head. "There's clever, boy. And then there's cocky."

That brought Yoshi down—but only a little. "If we save the world, no one will care how we did it. If we fail, there will be no one to care about anything."

"Then we had better succeed," Meru said.

"Yes," said Vekaa. "Now suppose you tell me what we are doing. Since there is no turning back."

It struck Meru then, hard enough to knock the breath out of her, how much he had trusted both of them. He had asked no questions. He had given them what they needed, let them do what they must, and only asked to be part of whatever they did.

That was more than trust. It was respect. Desperation, too, maybe. But he had given them a tremendous gift.

She gave back what she could. It was not much, but it was the best she had. "I cracked the code of my mother's message." No need for him to know how, or with whom, she had done it. "She was on her way to Egypt, to a certain place. A tomb. The body in it died of a plague."

"There are thousands of tombs in Egypt," he said, "and the newest of them is millennia old. Hundreds of the bodies in them died of illness. What does that have to do with an interstellar epidemic?"

"Maybe nothing," Meru said. "Maybe everything."

"And for that you enlisted this friend, who would be a starpilot with you and now will probably go down with you; broke a dozen laws; and endangered Consensus."

She bowed under the weight of that. "I didn't enlist him, he enlisted himself. But otherwise, yes. Would you rather I hadn't done anything, and let Earth die?"

"I would rather your mother were alive and you were safe on your way to be a starpilot," he said with an edge that made her flinch.

She straightened her back and firmed her voice. "There are thousands of tombs," she said, "but only one that held that particular scarab and the flower it was wrapped in. I think I know which one it was. I have to see it, to be sure."

He looked long and hard at her, studying her as if she had been one of the samples in his laboratory. Finally he said, "I'm going to trust you, just as I did my sister. She too did things that seemed illogical at the time, but they were always right in the end."

"Until they killed her," Meru said. Her voice was perfectly flat.

So was his. "That's why I'm letting myself be part of this. For her. To make her death count for something."

Meru's eyes stung with tears. She shook them off. "If I'm right," she said, "you can take what I find to Consensus. Then they can do what they need to do."

He nodded slowly. He did not ask what they would do if she was wrong.

She loved him for that. She would never say so, but as the bubble skimmed over the road, she moved closer to him and slipped her hand into his.

His fingers closed over hers. They were warm, and his clasp was firm. He would stay with her, it said. He would protect her as much as he could.

She was glad he was here. Not just for his skills and his clearances, either. He was family. He had loved Jian, too. And he loved Meru.

The shuttle port was crawling with security bots and crowded with Guards. They did not seem to be focusing on any shuttle in particular, but that was small comfort.

The starwing had shrunk to the smallest she had ever seen or known it to shrink, hardly larger than her outspread hand, and shifted phase until it was all but invisible. It wrapped around her wrist and clung.

Vekaa walked ahead of her, armed with his clearances, with Yoshi's enhancements. Yoshi walked just behind, still limping slightly. Bots and Guards moved out of their way.

Balance and confidence, Meru thought. She did her best to imitate them, to walk as if she had every right to be there.

The shuttle stood in a bay near the end of the port. Most of the other bays were closed and dark. The few that were open were empty.

They were going to be conspicuous when they left. Meru had hoped to hide herself in the welter of traffic, but everything had shut down. Nobody was traveling anywhere.

The shuttle was ready, open and waiting. Its course was set. All Meru had to do was get in, strap herself down, and let it go.

She stopped. "This could be a trap," she said.

Vekaa looked over his shoulder. "Not yet," he said. His voice was low and a little tight.

But soon there would be, he meant. Meru pushed herself back into motion, clinging as close as his shadow.

# Meru

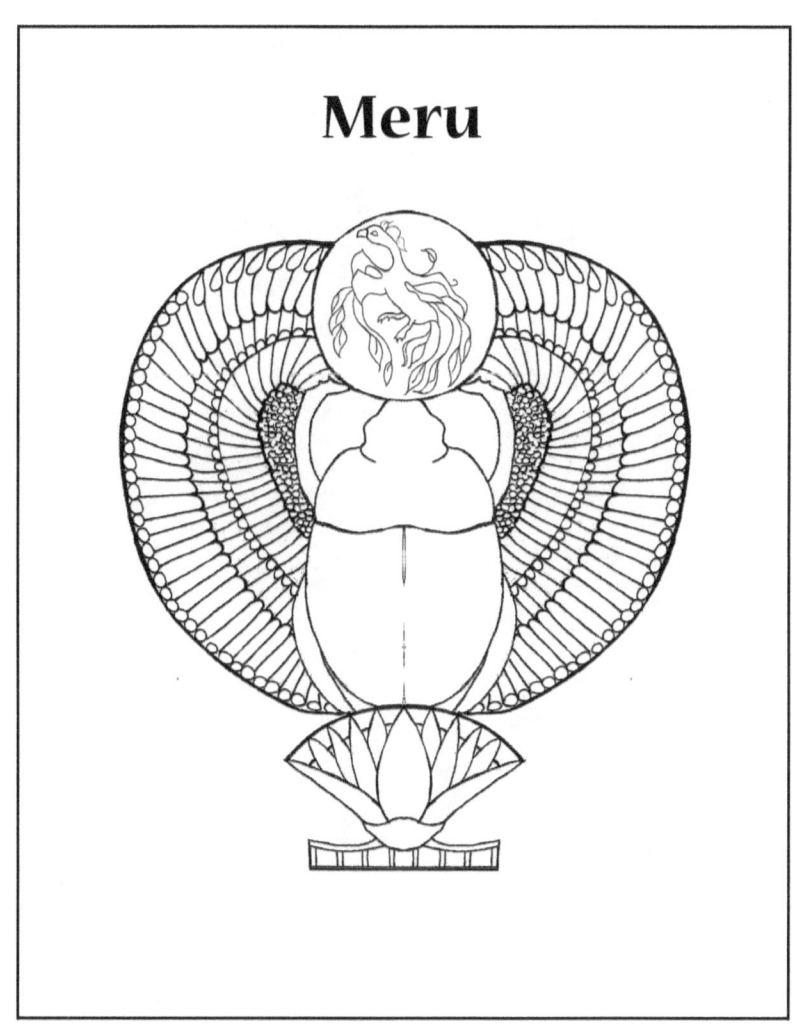

# Chapter 24

As Meru and Yoshi and Vekaa stepped from the walkway into the shuttle bay, the atmosphere in the port changed. Guards had drawn together. Bots swarmed around them.

One of the darkened bays opened, then another and another. Meru heard the unmistakable deep hum of shuttles readying for launch, multiplied more times than she could count, from end to end of the port.

They were all leaving—every one of them. Breaking Containment. Escaping the power of Consensus.

Vekaa caught Meru in one hand and Yoshi in the other and pulled them into the shuttle. He almost threw them into one of the double row of seats, and flung himself into the one opposite. "Strap in," he said, almost snapping it.

Meru and Yoshi obeyed without a thought of argument. Meru had hardly secured the last strap when the shuttle lifted: a faint tugging sensation and a popping in her ears.

The port shrank rapidly below them. Shuttles darted all around them, swarming like bees—that image came from Meritre, still present after all this time, and Meredith agreed with it. They were properly awed.

Meru turned to stare at Vekaa. He leaned back in his seat, eyes shut. There was a distinct grey cast under the warm deep brown of his skin.

"You didn't," she said.

His eyes opened. He looked angry and guilty and triumphant all at once. He reminded her, just then, of Yoshi—who was regarding him in open and astonished admiration. "We needed a diversion," he said.

"When they catch us," she said, "they'll lock us all up for the rest of recorded time."

"Not if we save the world," he said.

Under cover of the mass escape, the one shuttle that mattered to Meru soared from darkness into light. Then at last she saw below her the country that she knew as well as her family's island, though she had never seen it before in this life.

People still lived among the monuments, just as they had four thousand years ago, and four thousand years before that. There was a shuttle port; there were walkways through the newest parts of the city.

Instead of a ferry there was a force bridge across the river, a nearly invisible arch. People crossing looked as if they were walking on air.

The land of the dead was still much the same: the Red Land, bare and bleak, with its stark cliffs and barren valleys. There were more temples than Meredith had known, and many more tombs, each with its marker on the web. But in the world of the living, where human eyes could see, most of them were still hidden. No one had to dig any more, to know where a tomb or an artifact was. They had instruments that could see.

The Guards were out chasing empty shuttles and hunting down false trails. Here in ancient Luxor, three strangers were hardly worth noticing, unless they wanted to buy a scarab or a scarf or a skewer of something savory and spicy.

Meru kept a grip on the scarab that was hers three times over. The starwing had taken to the air again. It danced for a while with a hawk that hunted the coverts on the east bank of the river, then darted off westward.

She and Yoshi and Vekaa followed much more slowly. They were safe in the crowds, invisible and unremarkable. When those thinned, out past the clutter of houses and shops and museums that hugged the riverbank, they were still only three of many.

Meru had not expected to find so many people here. A notable number of them came from offworld. This was a great place of pilgrimage, it seemed; and with Earth on lockdown, they had nothing better to do than explore old monuments.

The walkway carried them to the edge of the Valley, but from there it was its old self: sandy, dusty tracks leading to temples and tombs. The sun was well up, and the heat with it. Meru's older selves well remembered the taste of it, sharp and dry.

She had relied on them to find the princess' temple for her. But all the tracks they knew had changed. There were so many temples, restored or rebuilt, and so many tombs that neither of them had ever known.

Meru had to try the web, though it might be a very bad idea. Through the starwing at least, she was harder to track.

She paused at the top of the hill. Vekaa handed her a bubble of water and a protein bar. She almost refused them, but both of her other selves had more sense. "You need fuel," Meredith said.

"And water," said Meritre.

Meru sat with Yoshi and Vekaa on a flat stone and ate and drank, and looked out across the valley. From this height it was like a map on the web, but without labels or markers.

It was still recognizable, if she focused on it. Meredith called this the Valley of the Queens. She knew where some of the tombs were, and whose they had been.

It was Meritre who stopped Meru's slow and almost despairing scan. "There!"

Meru blinked. She felt Meredith's frown. "What? Where?"

"There," said Meritre. She pointed, which was a strange sensation: like a shadow stretching out in front of Meru.

It stood a little apart from the other temples and the tomb entrances, near the sheer wall of a cliff. Someone had restored it: there were pillars and a roof. Gilding flashed in the sun.

"That is how it looks," Meritre said. "The colors, the gold—that's how it is."

"It's beautiful," said Meredith.

Meru was not thinking of beauty then. She was thinking of what had come out of it, and what it had done to people on so many worlds, and now was doing to Earth.

She tucked her half-empty bubble of water inside her suit, took a last bite of protein bar and swallowed it as she walked. She was aware of the others starting to ask what she was doing, then giving it up and simply following her.

It was not so easy once she was down in the valley, in the maze of tracks and temples. She aimed roughly where the princess' temple had to be.

The starwing hovered above her. It still could see what she had seen from the hill. With its help she mapped a course.

She was so focused on that that she forgot both of her companions. She remembered when Yoshi gripped her shoulder, stopping her short. "What is that? What are you doing?"

"What I need to do," she said.

He frowned. She braced for a fight, but he let her go.

"Later," Vekaa said, "you'll explain. In detail."

"Later," she agreed. With everything else that she had done, that was hardly anything to be afraid of.

For now, she had a route to follow. The knots of people turned to stragglers and then to sun-dazzled emptiness. There were just the three of them and the starwing, turning onto a track that, at last, her inner selves recognized. That precise angle of the cliffs, that tilt to the land, they knew. It had not changed.

The temple was smaller than Meru had expected. It was also closed off behind a force field. The seal of the Department of Antiquities was on it. *By permit only,* it said.

"Damn Department of Antiquities," Meredith said.

Meru laughed, because she wanted to cry. She could get in, but if she did, Vekaa would know how. And so, eventually, would Consensus.

It was all over for her anyway. She called the starwing down.

There was a brief, terrible moment when she was afraid it would not come; then when it came, that it could not shield all of them.

It stretched to cover them. Through it she felt Vekaa's shock and sudden burst of understanding—as if this answered a whole throng of questions. Yoshi was simply lost in the wonder and delight of it.

The force field hummed and crackled behind them. The temple stood open in front, with its gaudily painted façade and its court full of sunlight and shadow.

Meritre guided them all now. Through her memory Meru saw workers and scaffolding and heard the sounds of hammering, and saw a shadow kneeling in the corridor off to the right: slight, brown-skinned, with a smoothly shaven skull above a fine-boned face. He had a brush in his hand and a palette beside him, dotted with vivid colors.

He faded as Meru drew closer. The passage was empty.

She had no fear of shadows, but she shivered. It was deeply strange to live in three times at once.

Strange, and wonderful. She paused where the painted writing ended, and drew out the filter she had brought. Vekaa and Yoshi had already activated theirs, a slight but visible blurring of their features.

The scent of old stone and sunlit dust vanished. Meru breathed air scoured clean of any contaminant, down to the smallest virus.

She was glad of that safety, but sorry, too. So much of Egypt was in the air, in its smells and tastes. She missed it.

She would get it back. She walked down the passage, tracing Meredith's steps, and Meritre's before them.

She imagined that she could hear them walking with her, the sound of their feet magnified inside the square sandstone walls. She looked back, just as the light from above cut off, and one much harsher shot its glare down at her.

Consensus had found them.

Sanity would have stopped her there and made her wait docilely to be arrested. She was long past that. She spun and ran.

The other two were close on her heels. They could never outrun the Guards, and there was no exit, nothing below but, if her memory was true and not delusion, the princess' tomb.

She had come to find the tomb. She would find it. After that, nothing mattered.

# Meru

# Chapter 25

It was a long way down. Lights came on when the light from above gave out, soft and pale, just bright enough to guide Meru's feet.

The Guards seemed to have given up the chase. Why should they bother? She had to come out in the end, and they would be waiting.

Meru half wished the others would stop, too—but only half. The rest of her was glad to have them with her. It was unexpectedly cold down here, and dark, and dimmer than it should be. Even through the filter, the air felt heavy.

"Breath of the dead," Meritre said.

Meru had not needed to hear that. She pushed onward, grimly.

When it seemed that there would never be any end to that tunnel in the earth, it ended. Meru would not have been surprised to run into a blank wall, as Meredith's people had.

That was long gone. The stasis field was old, nearly as old as Meredith's time: it had an actual keypad, and physical controls.

Meru made no move to touch them. There was the *ka* statue, as bright and beautiful as the day it was set in its niche. There was the chamber, the ceiling of painted stars, the sarcophagus with its mask of the princess.

And there were the flowers, withered and faded, laid like a coverlet over the coffin. The rest, the banks of them that Meredith had seen with the camera, had disappeared. Scattered to the stars? It would seem so.

Meru drew out the one her mother had left for her. It lay in its own tiny stasis field, just as dry and just as withered as the ones in the tomb. "This is it," she said to Vekaa. "This is what you've been looking for."

She could still be wrong—hopelessly and catastrophically. She did not think so. Which was maybe arrogant of her. She was too tired to care.

He had instruments with him, not many, but enough to gather samples without breaking stasis. He had the web, too, with all its resources—and the Guards, when he called them down.

Officially they were all under arrest. In the circumstances, that meant little. Meru was glad this time to be taken off to Containment, because it meant a bath and clean clothes and real food, and a bed in which she could sleep like the dead.

When she woke, the sun's angle had hardly changed at all, but the web gave her a new date. She had slept straight into the next day.

The starwing was there, curled up next to her. Meritre and Meredith were awake inside her. When she searched the web for Vekaa, she found him nearby, in a lab, deeply engrossed in his work.

Yoshi was in the room, lying in a bed by the opposite wall, sound asleep. As she listened, she could hear his gentle snore.

"So I was right," she said to his oblivious back.

"You were right," Lyra said. She was sitting at the foot of Meru's bed, surrounded by the shimmer of the web. "Your mother guided you well."

It was not only her mother, Meru thought. Not at all. But she nodded. She did not have to feign the welling of tears. "Don't punish my uncle and my friend," she said. "I kidnapped them. I made them use my uncle's clearances. It's not their fault."

Lyra's brows lifted. "Really?"

"It's not," Meru said. "It's all me. I'm the one you need to punish."

"We owe you a great debt," said Lyra.

"I owe you an apology," Meru said, "and probably a prison sentence."

"You think so?" Lyra asked.

"I broke too many laws to count," said Meru.

"So you did," said Lyra. "You also found the source of the virus. The tomb in which it originated was one of the very first experiments in stasis, nearly four thousand years ago. At some point, perhaps several points, materials were removed from the tomb and preserved in their own, much smaller stasis fields."

"Flowers," Meru said.

"Flowers," Lyra agreed, "taken as remembrances and sold to collectors among the worlds. It was a fashion for a whole season, a craze that ran from end to end of human space. One of them, it seems, carried a fragment of the virus. But now we have the key. We have some hope of stopping it."

"I would hope for more," said Meru.

"So do we all," said Lyra.

She flickered and went out.

In a way Meru was disappointed. She had known better than to think that anyone could find a cure in a day. But she had dreamed that there was one, and Vekaa found it.

"Dreams can be true," Meritre said from the end of another plague, thousands and thousands of years ago.

"Then I'll try to keep on dreaming," said Meru, "and hoping, too. That they find the cure. That I haven't lost the stars. For me or for my friend."

"They owe you both for saving the world," Meredith said. "You can remind them that if they send you to starpilots' school, you'll be someone else's problem."

Meru laughed painfully. "That might actually work," she said.

"Can't hurt to try," said Meredith.

Certainly it could not hurt worse than anything else Meru had done or felt since her mother's message shook her out of her safe and comfortable world. She would try, she thought. She would do her best to succeed. After all, as Meredith said, she had saved the world.

# Meredith

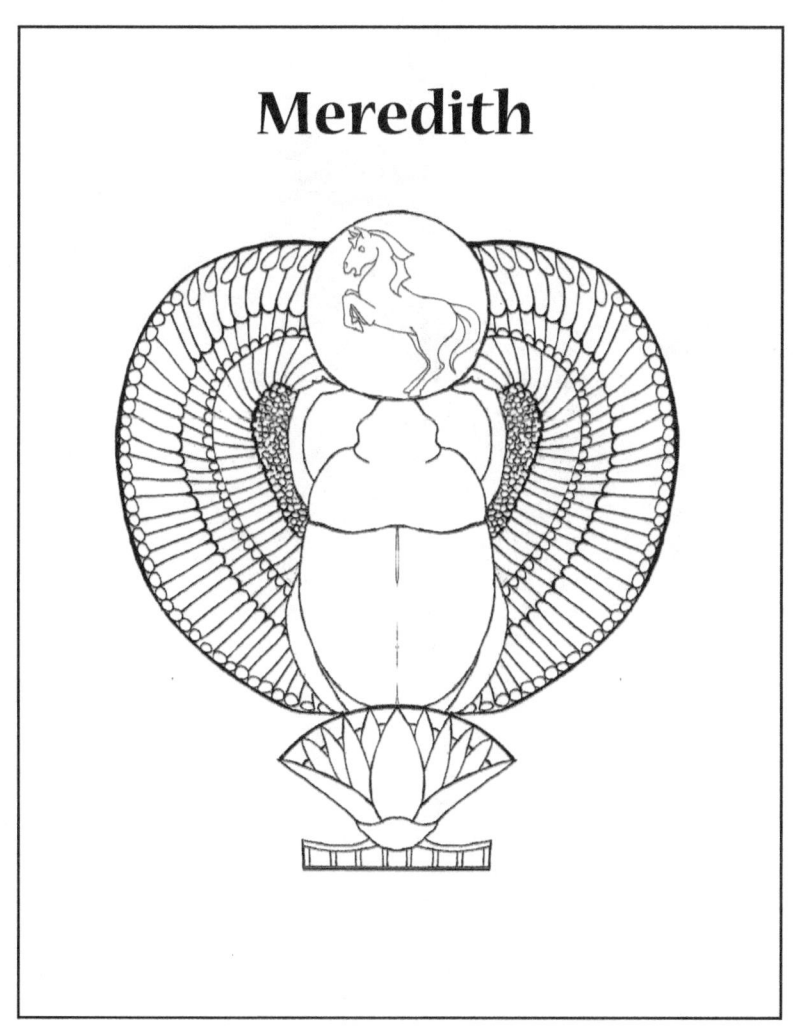

# Chapter 26

So that was what saving the world felt like. It felt empty.

Maybe it wasn't the flowers. Maybe it was all my fault. I might be carrying it right now, a string of molecules that would drift around the planet, replicating harmlessly, until one day it mutated. Then it mutated again and again, till one of the mutations turned toxic. After that, nobody could stop it.

Consensus would find a cure, now it knew exactly what it was dealing with. The epidemic would end; people would stop dying. Earth would be safe again.

I told myself Meru would be safe, too. She'd talk her way out of Containment and into starpilots' school, and get Yoshi out, too, and they'd end up sailing living ships across the stars. Meanwhile, on the other end of time, Meritre would sing the princess into her tomb, help her mother deliver the little brother or sister they all waited for with such fear and hope, marry her scribe and go on to live a long—for ancient Egypt—and happy life.

I could see their whole lives ahead of them, but when I looked at my own, I couldn't see past next week.

Maybe I was wrong, and all the huddling and whispering wasn't about Mom after all. Maybe I'd misheard. Maybe I was completely delusional.

Suppose I wasn't. Suppose Mom really wasn't going to make it. Dad and Aunt Jessie and Kelly had to figure out what to do with me.

They all had their own lives. Nobody wanted me. All I wanted was Mom.

I tried to call Mom, but she wasn't answering. Her voicemail was full.

I called Cat, and didn't even get to voicemail. *Out of service area*, the snide little voice buzzed in my ear. I started to punch a text, couldn't even get the words to make sense. I threw the phone across the room and pulled the covers up over my head.

There were still people inside it. Meritre and Meru didn't invite me to a pity party. They were just there, being me, the same way I couldn't help but be them.

Nobody ever said reincarnation was like that. You either got hypnotized and discovered you were Attila the Hun, or had weird memories that turned out to be from past lives. Remembering future lives, or being able to talk to yourself on either end, was straight off the edge.

"Meredith?"

Aunt Jessie usually sounds cranky when she's trying to be sympathetic. When she actually sounds sympathetic, that's not good at all.

I must have fallen asleep. I'd kicked the covers off and they were all twisted up at the foot of the bed. For a while I couldn't remember what day it was, or when I'd gone to bed.

It must be morning. I vaguely remembered it being dark, and now there was light through the blinds. The little tortie cat was curled up in her usual spot next to my pillow.

I rubbed the crusties out of my eyes. Aunt Jessie was wearing slacks and a blouse instead of dig clothes. "Is it Friday?" I asked.

She shook her head. Now she looked, as well as sounded, cranky. It didn't make me feel any better. "Meredith, I have something to tell you. If you'd rather have a shower and breakfast first—"

I sat up. My stomach had dropped around my ankles. "It's Mom, isn't it? Is she—"

"She went into a coma last night," Aunt Jessie said. "Your dad and Kelly left early this morning. You and I are flying out at noon. I'll help you pack."

I stared at her. What was swelling up in me didn't feel like anger. It felt like nothing I'd ever felt before. "What about the site? What about the tomb? You can't just leave it like that. You have to—"

"Meredith," she said. Sympathetic was bad, but quiet was worse. It cut me off in mid-rant. "Don't worry about it. It's all taken care of."

"What do you mean? Why didn't you wake me up? Why didn't you tell me? I could have gone with Dad and Kelly. What if we don't get there in time?"

Aunt Jessie's face looked made of wax. "They already had tickets for the day after tomorrow—they were able to get them changed. I got us the first flights we could get together. You needed to sleep, and there wasn't anything you could do. Now hurry up and get dressed while I pack your suitcase. We're leaving in an hour."

"It's already packed," I said.

She nodded. She didn't seem at all surprised. "Do what you need to get ready, then come down for breakfast. You're going to need it. We have a long trip ahead of us."

It took us most of two days to get to Florida. I don't remember much of it. When we were on the ground, Aunt Jessie was on the phone, checking in with the doctors and then with Dad and Kelly after they got there. In between those calls, she talked to Gwyn, whom she'd left in charge of the site, and Sayyid, who was keeping an eye on the passage and the tomb.

I didn't touch my own phone, much. When people called, I couldn't seem to find any words. After a while my friends said, "We'll see you when you get here." And left me alone.

Cat had got into the hospice. All she could tell me was what Aunt Jessie and Dad and Kelly had. And the other thing, the thing that mostly went without saying: *I'm here. I'll always be here. No matter what happens.*

I talked to Dad once, but somehow I felt better talking to Kelly. Maybe because she was almost a stranger, and a doctor, she knew how to put things so I didn't get them all messed up.

She didn't try to pretend that everything was going to be just fine. Not that even doctors can really predict, or miracles can't happen, but we all knew. This was it.

The Triple was useless. Meritre could pray if she wanted to. Meru was busy dealing with her own mother's death.

It did kind of help on those endless plane rides and those equally endless hours of waiting in airports, to either sit on the roof with Meritre and drink beer and eat Egyptian food, or roam the far-future web with Meru. Sometimes when I tried to sleep, I'd hear Meritre's cat purring, or else it was the starwing.

I missed the little cat from Luxor. I wondered if I'd ever see her again.

Sometimes I'd feel Bonnie close by. That was the one thing I looked forward to. If I was home, I could see Bonnie. I could bury my face in her mane and let go and cry till there were no tears left.

Mom was still alive when we got there. In the two weeks since I left, she'd gone from thin but apparently healthy to a stick figure in a hospice bed.

The hospice was nice. It was a house by the river, and the rooms were cool and quiet. Palm trees grew all around it; hibiscus bloomed along the walls and in the yard. There were orange and grapefruit trees, and a lemon tree beside the back door.

Mom's room looked down the river. She must have loved that while she was awake.

A big bouquet of roses sat on the table beside her bed. Cat's stepmom had acres of rosebushes, and these were some of Mom's favorites: all shades of lavender and yellow and white. They filled the room with a beautiful smell.

It almost covered the smell of cancer, that Meritre would call the smell of death.

Meritre was four thousand years dead. She was still alive inside me. But then *I* was dead compared to Meru.

How final is death, if you can come back and live a whole other life?

Final enough, I answered myself, for the people who love you in the life you're in. If Mom came back, she wouldn't be Mom any more. This was all I had of her, and all I'd ever get.

Cat had gone to the barn for morning chores. Aunt Jessie and Dad and Kelly were in the conference room talking to doctors. I was alone with Mom and the monitors.

Nothing in there was keeping her alive; she didn't want that. She had a little oxygen was all, and an IV with pain meds, to keep her comfortable.

That was how the nurses put it. "To keep her comfortable." By that they meant, so she wouldn't be in too much agony before she died.

Her hand felt like twigs wrapped in a thin leather glove. It was cold. I tried to warm it, but it was past that.

Maybe she knew I was there. People in a coma could hear, Kelly'd told me. That was why there was music playing, Mom's favorites: Beatles and show tunes and indie rock and medieval greatest hits.

Meritre was in the temple with the choir, while priests moved through a long and complicated ritual. Aweret wasn't the only person in that family with a wonderful voice. Meritre's made the small hairs lift on the back of my neck, it was so clear and high and perfect.

I couldn't even sing on key. But I could whisper the words in Mom's ear while the music mix shifted over to Anonymous 4. It all fit as if it was meant to: the voices, the words, the worlds and times all wound together—so far apart and yet so close.

Eight thousand years. Three lives, one soul. And all the lives and souls that we belonged to, or that belonged to us.

"*In every world I am with you*," I whispered while Meritre sang inside me and those four beautiful, almost supernatural voices echoed her in the still, dim room. On the other side of time I felt Meru, just being there, being part of us, and the starwing adding its weird sweet harmony.

> "*The cat slipping soft and supple through the door,*
> *two friends meeting by the river,*
> *sunrise and moonset and the paths of stars in the water—*
> *in all of those, I am with you. I speak to you.*
>
> "*I am the world and the world is in me.*
> *All that I am, I am for you.*
> *We are one, we who love.*
> *There is no death; there is no ending.*
> *We are one.*
> *We are all one, we who were, who are,*
> *who live in eternity.*"

I felt her go. Maybe my voice helped her, or showed her the way. Maybe she could hear that other voice, the one that was me, too, thousands of years ago, but still alive, still present, still here; and the voice that hadn't been born yet, that wouldn't be born for thousands of years.

One thing I know. She knew I was there. It could have been death making the signals misfire and the muscles twitch, but I felt her fingers tighten on mine.

They held for a handful of heartbeats. Then she was gone.

# Meredith

# Chapter 27

I've read the books. I know what I'm supposed to feel. Denial, anger, bargaining, depression, acceptance. See? I've got it memorized.

The bargaining part? If magic was real, that would work.

If magic was real, miracles would be, too. Mom would still be here.

Meanwhile, I settled right in the middle of anger, curled up and let it keep me warm. It was cold out there in the dark, no matter how many people came with cards and casseroles and bouquets of flowers.

They had tears. I couldn't find any. Dad and Aunt Jessie took care of things. Kelly took care of me, which I should probably have resented a lot, but I had too much else to be mad at.

That was a long night. People kept trying to make me go home, but I wouldn't. When morning came, the man from the mortuary came, too, to take Mom away.

Meritre's princess was still marinating in, basically, baking soda. Meru's mom was a vial of DNA and a bubble of ashes that they'd finally decided to scatter from a starship. My mom fit in the middle. DNA, no. Ashes, in a couple of days, yes.

That horrified Meritre so much she almost pulled out of the Triple. "You *burn* them? How can you do that? You've robbed them of eternity!"

"We've learned that it's not the body that lasts," Meru said. "It's the energy, the self—the thing you ancients call the soul. Look at us. Aren't we proof of it?"

Meritre didn't want to see that. It shook her whole world in ways we far-future selves couldn't really understand. Egypt is all about the mummies, if you ask most people in my time, and the mummies are about keeping every person's body whole so all her souls can last forever.

Everything else Meritre had seen about us was either so strange it didn't make enough sense to be a problem, or enough like things she knew that she had no trouble relating to it. This was right on the edge of unthinkable.

It distracted me, which wasn't an awful thing. The time I spent trying to figure out how to make Meritre feel better was time I wasn't facing the huge gaping hole in my life.

Mom used to be in that hole. Now she wasn't. The last place I wanted to go after the hospice was home to a house that was full of her things, her smell, her memories—but not her.

I could have made Dad or Aunt Jessie or Cat take me to a hotel. But I didn't. If Meritre could face a world that burned its dearest dead, I could face the house I'd lived in with Mom since I was five years old.

It wasn't home. Home had Mom in it. Sitting in the living room with the TV on but the sound off, gritting my teeth while friends and neighbors trooped through, I knew I could leave. Chicago, Massachusetts, Egypt—it didn't matter. This wasn't my house any more.

Nobody expected me to make much sense, and that was good, because I didn't have any to make.

Rick and Cat showed up in there somewhere—I think there was lunch on the table, or maybe it was supposed to be early dinner—and I was glad to see them, honestly. Rick brought a stack of movies for me to watch when I was up to it, and Kristen came loaded down with pizza, with Devon Mackey looming behind her.

Even in the state I was in, I could be impressed. For Kristen, three weeks was serious monogamy.

I wasn't much use to any of them. Tomorrow I'd be glad to watch movies or play online games or go riding with Cat and Kristen and a bunch of the barn kids. Today I'd slipped outside of time.

Even with Meritre gone off to deal with the shock to her system, I could open my eyes and see that fierce blue Egyptian sky. Or I'd look around and see stars, and hear the ocean crashing at the foot of Meru's favorite rock.

If it had been night, I'd have gone out on turtle watch. It was still hours until the sun went down. People kept coming and being sympathetic and bringing food. Food and funerals: that's been going on since long before Meritre, and from what I gathered from Meru, it was still happening thousands of years in the future.

Finally, when the sun had started to get low, the stream of people dried up. The usuals had families, dates, jobs to get to—all the things real people did when they had real lives.

Cat hung around the longest. "You sure you're okay?" she asked. "You don't need me to stay?"

"You'll be late for your shift," I said. "I'll be all right. I'll call you if I'm not."

"Promise?"

"Promise," I said.

"You better," she said. We aren't touchy types, but she hugged me, and held me for a long time, till I could hardly breathe. But I didn't care. I just wanted to stay where I was, forever and ever.

Finally she let me go. It was cold in the six inches between us, and lonely. "Tomorrow. We'll go for a ride in the orange grove."

"I'd like that," I said.

After that it was just us—and then it wasn't even that many. Dad and Aunt Jessie took off to do something at the mortuary—sign papers, pick out a casket, I wasn't paying attention. I could have gone with them, but I'd used up all my grit.

What I needed wasn't here. Kelly saw it, because she asked me, "What do you want to do? Can I help?"

I started to say no and hole up in my room, but I really needed to do this. If she was willing, why not? "I need to see Bonnie," I said. "My horse. Will you take me to the barn?"

I waited for her to say I should get some sleep instead, or point out that she was totally exhausted herself, but she didn't even blink. "Of course," she said. "Just tell me where to go."

I guess it's true about doctors working three days straight and still being able to function. Kelly grabbed the keys to the rental car—not Mom's car, which sat in the garage; Dad and Aunt Jessie hadn't taken it, either, and I was glad. I wasn't ready to see anybody else behind that wheel. Or worse, to be the driver with the learner's permit, and have someone else in the passenger seat.

It was a quiet ride. Kelly followed my directions, but aside from "Turn left" and "Go on a bit up there," neither one of us felt like making conversation.

The sun was almost down by the time we got to Mangrove Farm. A few people were around, mostly boarders who had day jobs and came to ride at night under the arena lights. It was a different world than the one I was usually in. I was a morning kid. These were the evening riders.

That was good. If they didn't know me, they couldn't crowd around and be all sympathetic. Barb wasn't in sight, and that was good, too. I just wanted Bonnie.

I pointed Kelly to the lounge with the air conditioning and the vending machines. By the time she opened the door, I was halfway past the barn to Bonnie's pasture.

Usually when I went on vacation, Bonnie wouldn't speak to me when I came back. I'd get a prime view of her backside, and that's the best I'd get for three days.

This time I saw her backside, all right, but that's because she was nose down in her evening hay. When I rattled the chain on the gate, her head popped up and she did the neatest pirouette you'll ever see, and cantered over to me.

I don't cry for humans. I cry for things that are so beautiful I just can't stand it, like Bonnie in front of me, all crusty from rolling in the sand, with a mouthful of half-chewed hay and eyes that knew everything I'd ever thought or felt or been.

Impatient Bonnie, who always has to be moving and thinking and doing, stood for a long time while I cried into her mane. Her warm animal smell filled my nose.

The other two inside touched her through me with a kind of wonder. Meritre had never seen or heard of a horse. For Meru it was a creature she'd seen on the web, that still existed outside of Earth, but the real thing was more than she could have imagined. For her, Bonnie was as wonderful as the starwing.

She really was. I hugged her firm silky neck and scritched her favorite spots, all around the withers and down the front of her shoulders. She hugged me back, pressing me to her chest for a minute before she let go.

While I was with her, finally I was home. I could feel Mom around us, because Mom loved her so much, and that was Mom's baby in her, growing slowly the way horse babies do.

If I went to Chicago, what would happen to Bonnie? Where would she go? Would I ever see her again?

I couldn't be thinking these things tonight. But I had to. I had to think of so much, and I had to do it soon. It wouldn't go away.

Bonnie shook her head and blew, stamping at the flies. I raised my head from her mane and blinked. It was getting dark.

I couldn't believe I'd been out there that long. The sun was down and the moon was coming up.

It was doing the same thing over Meritre's stone and mud-brick city and Meru's cold ocean. Meritre had the cat in her lap. Meru was wrapped in the starwing. We were all together, remembering our dead.

It wasn't a sad feeling. That was kind of weird, but kind of comforting. Bonnie was there for all of us, big and white and calm.

There was hope inside her. I moved down the length of her and rested my head on her big white butt. My hand rested where the baby must be.

It was 'way too little to feel yet, but it was alive and moving around in there. Mom had a magazine that showed what it looked like, from someone who ran a camera into a mare's uterus. It looked like a horse, with legs and ears and eyes and everything, even this tiny. And it galloped—up and down in its own private ocean.

I swear I could see it. Meru could, too, on her web, and Meritre because we could. That was life, as alive as it could possibly be.

Death never wins. It knocks you flat and finishes you off, but you wake up again. You come back.

That's what we were. We'd changed something because of it. We'd helped save Meru's world.

I still wanted to scream and howl and throw rocks at the walls because I wanted my Mom back. That wouldn't let up any time soon. But I didn't want to be dead with her, whatever that was in between the me I was and the me I'd be when I was Meru. This world, with sand in my shoes and horse smell in my hair and a mosquito taking a big, bloody bite out of my elbow, was— is—the best thing there is.

That's why Meritre's people wanted to take everything, body and all, into the afterlife. They weren't about death and mummies and tombs. They were about life. They loved it so much, they never wanted to let it go.

Tears wouldn't stop running down my face. They blurred the moon until it was all one wide white glow across eight thousand years. And there was Bonnie right in the middle, whiter and stronger than anything.

I hugged her tight. I hugged the life that was in all of us. Then I went to deal with all the things you have to deal with when someone you love dies, because that's part of life, too. It's the price you pay for being alive.

# About the Author

**Judith Tarr** holds a PhD in Medieval Studies from Yale. She is the author of over three dozen novels and many works of short fiction. She has been nominated for the World Fantasy Award, and has won the Crawford Award for *The Isle of Glass* and its sequels. She lives near Tucson, Arizona, where she raises and trains Lipizzan horses.

# About Book View Café

**Book View Café** is a professional authors' cooperative offering DRM-free ebooks in multiple formats to readers around the world. With authors in a variety of genres including mystery, romance, fantasy, and science fiction, Book View Café has something for everyone.

**Book View Café** is good for readers because you can enjoy high-quality DRM-free ebooks from your favorite authors at a reasonable price.

**Book View Café** is good for writers because 95% of the profit goes directly to the book's author.

**Book View Café** authors include Nebula and Hugo Award winners, Philip K. Dick and Rita award winners, and *New York Times* bestsellers and notable book authors.

www.bookviewcafe.com